MW01228078

LANCE STAR
SKY RANGER
IN

The Crown of Gengis Kai

BOBBY NASH

First BEN Books Printed Edition 2021

WWW.BEN-BOOKS.COM

Lance Star and The Crown of Gengis Kai
A Lance Star: Sky Ranger adventure

© 2021 Bobby Nash
All Rights Reserved.

Book Production and design by Bobby Nash.
Edited by Ben Ash Jr.
Cover Art: James Burns

ISBN: **9798729505197**

Printed in the USA

Published by BEN Books
PO Box 626, Bethlehem, GA 30620
WWW.BEN-BOOKS.COM

And so it begins…

Dedicated to Air Chiefs Ron Fortier and Rob Davis, who first introduced me to the word "pulp" and were instrumental in bringing Lance Star and his Sky Rangers to life in the first place. Keep flyin' high, gents.

There aren't many men that Lance Star would drop everything and fly halfway around the world for, but a cryptic letter from his old friend asking to meet was enough to pique the air ace's interest.

An hour later, Lance, accompanied by his trusty chief of staff, Buck Tellonger, was airborne in one of their unmarked cargo planes.

"Any particular reason we're not taking the ol' Skybolt this time around?" Buck asked, referring to Lance Star's most famous creation and the plane everyone associated with the air ac and his crew.

"We have to keep this one under the radar," Lance said. As usual, he was doing the flying while Buck kicked back and enjoyed the ride. Normally, he would have served as navigator, but his friend hadn't told him where they were going yet.

"Ah, one of *them* deals," Buck said around a toothy grin just before popping one of those big, cheap, smelly cigars he loved so much into his mouth. "A favor for the general again?"

General Walter Pettigrew, in addition to being a longtime friend of the Star family, was also the liaison between the United States Air Corp and the Sky Rangers. On occasion, the general called on the Sky Rangers for a mission or twelve.

"Not this time, Buck."

Buck leaned back in his seat and puffed on his charoot.

"Then who?"

"Do you remember me mentioning Professor Simon Prentiss?"

Buck rubbed his chin as he tried to recall the name. "It does ring a bell, but I can't place him. He's an old school chum, right?"

"That's him," Lance said. "We were roommates for a couple of semesters in college. We got on all right, had an adventure or three together before he went off to study abroad and I joined the Air Corp."

"What did he end up studying?"

"Simon's a digger. He got his doctorate in archaeology. He's discovered some pretty interesting treasures in all corners of the world."

"Fascinating."

"Agreed," Lance said. "He sent a telegram saying that he was onto something big and needed a helping hand. He asked me to meet him."

"Any idea why?"

"None, but he said it was urgent," Lance said.

"And that worries you?" Buck stated matter-of-fact.

"Yeah. That's what worries me," Lance agreed.

"You think he's in trouble?"

"I really don't know, Buck. The boy sure does like digging in the dirt. Not sure how much trouble that can get you into, but you know how easy it is for trouble to come knocking."

"I guess it depends on whose dirt he's digging around in," Buck said.

"Agreed."

"We've all got our quirks. Your friend likes digging in the dirt. We like getting elbow deep in mechanics grease and burnt oil. It takes all kinds, huh?"

"And we've been known to get into trouble without even trying, is that what you're getting at?"

"Who, me?" Buck said, feigning innocence. For all of the big man's bluster, he was a thinker. More than one man has had a bad day because he underestimated Buck Tellonger.

Buck sat up straight and plucked the cigar from his teeth. "Maybe it's time you told me where we're headed," he said.

"Of course, Buck. It's no big secret. We just have to be careful is all. Simon asked that we keep this meeting under the radar. He doesn't want to attract any undue attention."

"Hence, no Skybolt."

"Exactly. We fly the Skybolt into this place and everyone will know who we are, and it won't be long before our friends with the cameras show up and start snapping our photos."

"Damn reporters," Buck muttered.

"Exactly," Lance said. As a celebrity, whether he thought of himself that way or not, Lance was a well-known public figure and therefore his movements were newsworthy. Staying off the press's radar was the only way a man like Lance Star could move around freely.

"The trials and tribulations of being the universally beloved Lance Star: Sky Ranger," Buck joked, returning the cigar for another puff.

"There are enough guys who have tried to kill me to disprove that universally loved bullpucky," Lance said. "But I take your point. That's why we're arriving in this unmarked model. She's nothing anyone will give a second look at, but she's still fully loaded with all the usual goodies just in case we need to shoot our way out of there."

"Now that you've danced around that answer, I'll ask again… where are we headed, Lance?"

"Are you familiar with the island nation of Magnapor?"

LANCE STAR

SKY RANGER

THE CROWN OF GENGIS KAI
WRITTEN BY BOBBY NASH

1.

"Magnapor?"

Caught off guard by the unexpected answer, Buck Tellonger nearly choked on his odiferous cigar. He coughed up a puff of noxious smoke.

"You mean the island?" he asked around a cough.

"That's the place," Lance said, enjoying his friend's discomfort. "I see you've heard of it."

"Yeah. You could say that, Chief. Calling Magnapor a cesspool is an insult to cesspools everywhere. That place is full of thieves, murders, and despots. Not the kind of place nice, civilized folks like you and me should be messing about, if you get my drift. This place makes Scavenger Quay look like an old folk's home, for goodness sakes."

Having barely escaped from Scavenger Quay once, himself, Lance laughed at the comparison.

"So, you are familiar with it then?" Lance said again.

"I may have made a pit stop there once or twice back in my wilder days," Buck admitted. "That's not something I usually brag about, mind you, but you asked me specifically to come along on this trip. How did you know I knew the lay of the land?"

"You like to talk when you drink, Buck."

"I do not!" the burly bulldog said with so much authority that his handlebar mustache all but stood at attention.

Before entering the service as a combat pilot back in the Big War, Buck had worked the private sector as a cargo pilot. Even though he handled legitimate cargo runs, Buck had also dabbled in less than legal enterprises to make ends meet. Times were tough and he couldn't afford to be choosy with his clients. Those smelly cigars of his might have been cheap, but Buck Tellonger had a voracious appetite, as his ever-expanding waistline demonstrated. He had also grown accustomed to living indoors. That required an influx of cash.

It was this story he had once told Lance after a night out on the town and they had drank a bit more than they should have. When the party died down, the flyboys took the party on the road and ended up drinking as they sat around a campfire near Lance's cabin at Star Field. Buck had mentioned his time flying in and out of Magnapor island when he worked as a smuggler for a time. Lance tucked the tidbit away for a rainy day.

Today's forecast called for intermittent showers.

After the war, instead of returning to the business he had left behind, Buck came to work for Lance when the younger pilot started up his new business, a company simply named Lance Star, Incorporated. Like Buck, Lance Star was an air ace himself, having flown numerous missions both on and off the books. His goal for peacetime was to build a line of cargo planes for civilian clients and fighter planes for the United States government.

Utilizing his family's land, left to Lance when his father passed away, they broke ground their second day back home from the fighting. The first day back, they got hammered as they roamed from one welcome home party to end of the war party, and back again.

An only child, Lance inherited the land that was now home to Star Field, a small, fully functioning private airfield in upstate New York. Once the airfield was built, Lance and his team went to work constructing a manufacturing space and several hangars to park the planes once they were completed. Small cabins lined the far end of the field, homes for Lance and his team, known across the world as the Sky Rangers. Some of the

Sky Rangers kept homes outside of Star Field, but Lance made sure they each had a place to crash on those long nights when heading into the city after work was the last thing they wanted to do.

Lance Star, Incorporated and Star Field each proved successful and self-sustaining. Lance was the boss, but he wasn't a meetings and boardroom kinda guy so he made Buck Tellonger his chief of staff. They then offered the day to day running of the place to Walt Anderson. Walt was a pilot himself, but could no longer fly due to an injury he received in combat with Baron Otto Von Blood, an old enemy of the Sky Rangers and a constantly recurring thorn in their side.

With Walt sidelined, Lance appointed him operations manager. It was a tough job, but Walt took to it like a duck to water. Before long, he had things running at peak efficiency and kept the cogs moving. As far as Lance was concerned, the position was Walt's as long as he wanted it.

With Walt Anderson running things, that left Lance and Buck with time to do what they loved, build and fly airplanes.

Magnapor was roughly the size of Hawaii. The small island country was a patchwork of clashing ideologies. One side of the island was comprised completely of farmland, forest, and jungle. Several types of livestock were raised as well as crops planted and cultivated year-round, thanks to the island's tropical climate. There was never a fear of a winter freeze, but the odd hurricane was a legitimate concern.

The other side of the island sported a modern city about half the size of Chicago. Skyscrapers stretched high into the sky, offering those who could afford to live and work in them expansive views of the island and the sea that surrounded them. The locals called it the *Emerald City*, an obvious comparison to the city from

The Wizard of Oz, one of Lance's favorite books. The green glass on the tallest skyscrapers only amplified the appellation.

From the outside looking in, Magnapor was paradise incarnate. For those who lived there, however, Magnapor was a struggle for survival. The Black Market surged on the island. Smuggling had become a bigger export than the island's many varieties of fruit and vegetables. Many of the inhabitants, especially in the urban areas, were poor, hungry, and living in the streets under the shadows of half a million-dollar high rises.

The government was no help. Magnapor was ruled by a prince, who led, not by example, but with an iron fist. A cabinet of ministers governed in name only. The prince kept them on a short leash so he could continue to profit of the hard work and misery of his subjects living below. Nothing happened on the island that did not kick back a cut to the throne.

Everyone knew better than to get on the prince's bad side.

Lance lined up on approach and stared at their destination. In front of him stood a major metropolitan city surrounded by jungle. One building stood far taller than the others, its green glass sparkling against the sunlight.

"Would you look at that?" Lance said.

"That, my friend, is the home of the islands *Overlord*. He lives in the penthouse and likes to look down on his subjects from on high," Buck said. "It would be in our best interest to avoid him and his flunkies."

"I'll do my best, Buck."

"You need to take this place serious, boss. Magnapor ain't Hell, exactly, but it's pretty darn close.

"I read ya." Lance pointed. "And that?"

"The volcano? Yeah. That's a nice conversation starter. A volcano in the heart of a jungle. Impressive, no?"

"Sounds like something out of a storybook," Lance said. "I take it, it's…"

"Oh, it's active," Buck confirmed. "But has not erupted in a long time. It should be safe."

"Should be…" Lance started. "When have we ever set foot on a volcano and it not erupt? Our luck doesn't fly that way, Buck. You know that."

"First time for everything, boss."

Lance shot his friend a dirty look, but before he could say anything, Magnapor's control tower chimed in, and interrupted their friendly duel.

"This is Magnapor tower to incoming aircraft. Please state you call numbers and destination."

"Magnapor control, this is NG-387," Buck said into the headset microphone. "Request landing clearance."

Long seconds ticked by as they waited for the tower chief to get back to them. Lance had landed in more airports than he cared to count and none of the tower controllers ever seemed to be in any sort of rush to get the planes on the ground. Once you were on the ground, however, you couldn't move fast enough to please them.

"You are cleared for landing, NG-387," the tower finally said. "Follow to runway two and stay on marker."

"Copy that, tower. On marker. We have the stick."

"See you on the ground, NG-387. Welcome to Magnapor."

"Welcome to Magnapor," Buck parroted with a nod and a wink after he disconnected the call.

Lance couldn't help but laugh.

A short time later, Lance and Buck closed and locked their rented hangar across from the landing strip. Lance had rented the space under the name of Rodney Knight, an alias he used on occasion. Once the plane was secured, they washed up, changed clothes, grabbed their gear, and headed toward the gate where they hoped to catch a taxi to take them into the Emerald City.

What neither of the air aces noticed was the man hiding in the shadows, watching them. He wore a dark suit, a frumpy jacket, a hat, and a dark tie. He would have blended completely into the shadows cast by the setting sun had he not decided to light a cigarette.

When the taxi picked them up a few minutes later, the man watched them leave.

A second later, an unmarked car pulled to the curb and he got inside.

"Follow them," he told the driver.

2.

"That'll be five bucks," the cab driver said once they arrived at their destination.

"Five dollars?" Buck Tellonger groused even as he pulled five crumpled one-dollar bills from his shirt pocket. "That's highway robbery, pal!"

"Just pay the man," Lance Star said as he opened the door and climbed out of the cab into the humid clime and immediately felt sweat begin to rise on his forehead.

"Many thank yous, sir," the cabbie said playfully as Buck passed over the cash. The local brandished a phony accent even as he flashed a crooked smile to his customers. In an exotic tourist trap like Emerald City, graft was everywhere, and prices were gouged to match. Had the cab driver known who they were, the price probably would have doubled or tripled.

"Five bucks," Buck said for a third time once they were standing on the sidewalk outside. "That's highway robbery. Why, I've half a mind to walk back to the airfield when we're finished here."

"In this heat?" Lance asked, wiping his forehead once more. "Be my guest."

"Well... maybe not," Buck agreed, dabbing a handkerchief against his own sweaty brow.

Emerald City had looked like an island paradise from above the clouds. On the ground, it reminded Lance of a flea market or a bazaar out of an old Saturday serial with banners hanging everywhere and hucksters pushing their wares on unsuspecting visitors. He doubted the city was a safe place to be a tourist and instinctively touched his wallet to make sure it was securely zipped into shoulder pocket of his flight suit he wore beneath the flight jacket that he was roasting inside of at the moment. Despite the heat, the jacket stayed in place.

Buck described the city bazaar as a den of thieves, a haven for ne'er-do-wells and Lance was beginning to see what his friend was talking about. At ground level, Magnapor's Emerald City was filled with the poor and those who preyed on them. Meanwhile, the green-tinted glass of the Overlord's tower stretched high into the heavens, towering over the city and its inhabitants.

Lance decided he didn't care much for the Overlord. He was the kind of villain that the Sky Rangers routinely faced off against. However, as much as he might wish to introduce himself, Simon Prentiss' message had advised discretion so he bit down on his anger and focused on the task at hand.

"I'm thinking we need a place with air conditioning," Lance said matter-of-fact. He pointed toward the address they had been given.

"Good luck," Buck told him. "I bet only a third of the buildings here have reliable electricity, much less functioning air conditioners."

Lance gave him a look that asked if he was being serious.

"I told ya, pal. Magnapor ain't Hell, but it's darn close."

"Let's find this place and get out of the heat," Lance said, pulling the name of the place his friend had set aside to meet.

The streets were still wet from an earlier rain storm that left tiny rivers flowing along the raised sidewalks. The sun was slowly setting behind the mountains to the west, casting the sky in a fiery concert of reds, oranges, yellow, blues, and purple that would soon slip silently into darkness. Like several large metropolises back in the states, Emerald City rarely slept. Colored lights and tiki torches flared to life, casting colorful murals on the walls and makeshift bazaar shops.

It almost looked beautiful lit up in such a manner.

Lance pointed. Up ahead stood a rough and tumble dive bar with a flashing neon sign above the entrance that read *Great And Powerful*, another not-so-subtle nod to Baum's classic tale. The *e* and *r* on the garish neon sign were burnt out so it read *Great And Pow   Ful* in all caps.

That was the place where Lance and Buck were headed.

"You sure this is the place?" Buck asked.

"That's the address," Lance said, handing over the telegraph to his friend.

Shaking his head, Buck verified the address. "Not exactly the kind of place I'd expect to find a world-renowned archaeologist."

Lance chuckled and took back the slip of paper and returned it to his inside jacket pocket. "Simon always said he would brave the gates of hell if it meant finding whatever treasure he was looking for," the air ace said. "I guess he wasn't kidding."

"Apparently not."

"Visit scenic Magnapor," Lance joked as he headed toward the front door.

"Better watch your wallet," Buck muttered and followed.

After slipping a couple of dollars a piece to the doorman who was built like a tank Buck had once fire-bombed during the war, they stepped inside the old Great and Powerful. The place was standing room only and loud music blared from the live band tucked away in the far corner. The air was filled with a mixture of sweat, booze, and old cigars that smelled worse than the el cheapo brand Buck smoked.

The club's regulars were a who's who of rough and rowdy sailors, smugglers, thieves, and assorted scoundrels.

"Are you sure this is the right place?" Buck asked. He was starting to get that old familiar tingle at the back of his neck that warned him he was about to get into a fight.

"This is where Simon said he would meet us, Buck," Lance assured his friend. "What can I say, his danger radar doesn't work like yours or mine."

"Obviously not," Buck agreed. "Mine told me not to step foot inside this dump. I don't like it, boss."

"Too rough for you?" Lance asked with a snarky grin.

"I don't mind a rough 'n tumble pub, but this place reminds me of a powder keg. one wrong spark—" Buck snapped his fingers. "—and boom!"

"Lance!" a voice shouted from somewhere in the crowd.

Lance Star looked for his friend, but did not see him.

"Lance!" Simon Prentiss shouted again and this time he walked out of the smokey haze where his friend could see him clearly.

As always, Simon was all smiles. Lance could only recall a handful of times during college when Simon had gotten a little miffed, much less out and out angry. He was the happiest guy the pilot had ever met, unless hidden antiquities were involved. He took the stealing of historical finds very personal. Lance once broke up a fistfight between the young Mr. Prentiss and a college professor who he claimed was stealing and selling antiquities that the college museum had paid him to find to private collectors.

Lance reached out a hand and his friend shook it.

"Lance Star, you old sky jokey! How have you been, old buddy?"

"Still airborne!" Lance said and pulled the man into a bear hug, clapping him on the back. "Good to see you, pal!"

"You too," Simon said loudly after pulling back from the hug. "It's been way too long. Thanks for coming."

"You called. I'm here," Lance stated. He pointed toward his co-pilot. "Simon Prentiss, let me introduce you to Buck Tellonger. Buck is an ace pilot, second in command of the Sky Rangers, and all-around nice guy. I mean, he's not as good a pilot as me, but who is?" Lance joked.

"A pleasure to meet you," Buck said, offering a hand and a smile to the new acquaintance while offering side-eye to his boss.

"Likewise. Any friend of Lance's is a friend of mine, Mr. Tellonger."

"Buck, please," he said, waving away the formality.

"Buck it is then. I'm Simon."

Simon and Lance were about the same age, only a few months apart, at best, but years out in the sun and digging up ancient civilizations had prematurely aged Simon. He looked about five years older than his former college roommate. His skin was perpetually tanned from constant exposure to the elements, burnt like worn leather around the neck and forearms. His black hair was cut short, only a few centimeters all around, which made sense for someone who lived the bulk of his life outdoors where hair tended to get in the way.

"Come on," Prentiss said. "I've got us a table in the back so we can talk."

He ushered the pilots through the crowd to a small table along the back wall. The booth was a semi-circle with a table in the center. Bean-covered strings hung from the ceiling around the table. It was the closest the crowded pub could offer to a private booth.

Simon held up a three fingers to the waitress, who nodded.

"Please…" Simon said and motioned for his guests to take a seat.

Before the could get comfortable, the waitress sat a pitcher of draft on the table along with three frosty mugs. She took away the glass Simon had been drinking from before his guests arrived.

"Nice place," Buck offered.

"I've drank in worse," Simon said as he poured a round for everyone.

"So have I," Lance and Buck said in unison.

They laughed.

Lance took a draw off of his beer. It was cold. "Not that it's not good to see you, Simon, because it's damn good to see you, son, but what was so urgent you had to drag us halfway around the world?"

"I found it," Simon said.

Lance's smile faded. He sat his mug back on the table.

"I found it, Lance," Simon said again before his friend could say anything.

"Oh, Simon…"

"I mean it this time, Lance. I found it!"

"You meant it last time too."

"That was different, Lance, and you know it!"

"No! I don't know it!" Lance said. "You know why I don't know it?"

"Found what?" Buck asked.

The two old friends ignored him as they continued a very old argument.

"Don't say it," Prentiss warned.

"It's a myth, Simon! The bloody thing doesn't exist!"

"What doesn't exist?" Buck asked.

"Why did you think I called you?" Prentiss asked.

"I don't know. Maybe you missed me and wanted to catch up, talk old times?" Lance shouted. Some sailors from another table turned their direction and Lance waved them off.

"What is it you've found? Buck asked again, a bit more forcefully this time.

Simon looked at his old friend as if asking silent permission.

Lance sighed. "Go ahead," he said and motioned for Simon to proceed.

"I've located The Crown of Gengis Kai."

"I'm sorry. You've found the what now?" Buck asked.

"I'm not surprised you aren't more familiar with Gengis Kai, Mr. Tellonger? His story is rarely told in the West."

"We're going to need more drinks for this," Lance said, polishing off the last of the beer.

He waved down the waitress.

"You never were much of a believer, were you?" Simon asked.

"In what?" Lance asked. "Simon, I admire your conviction, but Gengis Kai is nothing more than a legend, a story made up to scare kids. He's a bogeyman, nothing more. He didn't exist and neither did his crown. This Crown you've spent your whole life looking or is nothing more than a treasure hunt, a snipe. I'm sorry, pal, but there's no evidence the guy or the crown ever existed."

"History is rife with unproven theory, Lance. At least until it is proven true. The world was flat until someone proved it wasn't. Earth was the center of the universe until someone proved it was not. Dinosaurs did not exist until someone dug up the bones of once. Man was never meant to fly until someone proved they could."

"He's got you there, boss," Buck said, needling the point.

"Simon, I admit, it's a great story, but that's all it is, a story. If there was any truth to it, don't you think you would have found it by now."

Simon Prentiss smiled.

"Sonuvabitch," Lance said. "You actually found something, didn't you?"

"Maybe."

"Let's see it!"

"Perhaps a little context for those of us who haven't a clue what you're talking about would be nice," Buck Tellonger said.

Lance summoned the waitress again.

"We are definitely going to need more drinks.

The two men who followed Lance Star and Buck Tellonger from the airfield took a seat not far from the pilots and their friend. From their table, they couldn't hear what the men were discussing, though the occasional word or two floated by loud enough to discern. Whatever they were talking about, the discussion grew heated for a moment before their voices returned to neutral.

In a city like Magnapor, a place where only a few laws existed, these men were the law. They were agents of The Overlord, the man who ruled the island with an iron fist most of the time, but with a boot when excess force was required. Working for The Overlord was a privilege, one only open to a select few.

These two men, Agents Smith and Jones, obvious aliases, were part of that select number. They were ruthless, like their boss. Agents carried out the whims of The Overlord. His will was law.

Magnapor locals knew better than to cross these men. An Agent had full authority to do whatever they wanted, so long as it did not contradict or cross the man who lived above int eh emerald tower. The locals gave them whatever they wanted and tried to stay out of the line of fire.

Getting into club Great and Powerful was child's play with their badges. When they picked out the table they wanted, the group who had been sitting there, vacated it quickly.

"Are you certain that is him?" Jones asked, watching their quarry.

"Yes. There can be little doubt," Smith replied.

"Excellent."

"Yes," Jones said. "He is the target."

3.

Lance Star had heard this story before.

He did not relish the idea of hearing it again, but he knew it was inevitable. It was Simon Prentiss' favorite tall tale, after all. Lance had never believed a word of it, though he was in the minority when Simon and Lance's late father got together. The elder Star had also been a believer.

Sometimes, Lance wondered if his resistance to accept the story at face value was because his father had so readily done so. Even now, with everything he had seen, and the Sky Rangers had encountered more than their fair share of unnatural events, things that strayed outside the norms, or out and out should not have existed.

Why was this flight of fancy where he drew the line?

"You're not familiar with Gengis Kai, Mr. Tellonger?" Simon was saying. "Not surprising. His story is rarely told in the west. Kai was a mystic warrior. Legend has it that he tamed these islands by fighting back not only hordes of hostile locals, but also standing against the gods of fire and lava as well."

"Fascinating," Buck said, clearly caught in the same spell that had captured the imagination of Simon and Lance's father.

"As the myth goes," Simon continued. "Kai was the only mortal to ever best the Warriors of Hades in combat."

"I'm not familiar with them."

"I wouldn't expect you to be," the professor said. "Long ago, they ravaged these islands and beyond, terrorizing the inhabitants..."

Long ago and not so far away...
Gengis Kai stood on the deck of his ship and surveilled his kingdom. A tall, muscular man, he stood roughly six foot six. His long, black hair was tied into a tail and his thick beard was similarly woven on his face. His dark hair stood out in stark contrast to the crown of gold that adorned his head. The crown was rumored to contain powerful magic, controlled by the wearer through the amethyst gem embedded in the golden band. Several large leaves added an impressive plumage to the covering he wore beneath the crown, itself a velvety purple to match the shine of the powerful gem that sat on his forehead, an inch above his eyes.

For years, Gengis Kai had pillaged the tiny island nations of the South Pacific. He had even ventured to the mainland where he had aced down his enemies in their strongholds. He had amassed treasures greater than any pirate before him and had conscripted armies into his service to protect those baubles and the land where they were kept for the day Gengis Kai might return to claim them.

His real name lost to the mists of time, the man who gave himself the name Gengis Kai became a legend. His name was known from one corner of the globe to the other, even in lands where he had not stepped foot, his legend preceded him.

A legend built on fear.

Gengis Kai was the boogeyman that parents warned their unruly children about and it was a role he relished playing. The world, he believed, required a ruler with a strong fist to run it.

He planned to be that strong fist.

To most who had encountered him, Gengis Kai was a tyrant, stealing what he needed and taking things he wanted, whether it me food, gold, mead, property, men, or women. Kai denied himself nothing. He worked hard to claim the territory he owned, and he enjoyed the spoils of those victories. Kai was a man of great appetites.

The men and women who served under his iron rule were well taken care of, which bought their loyalty and fealty. Their bellies, purses, and beds remained full, as did their appetite for new conquests. There were always new challenges to face and overcome.

Gengis Kai loved a good challenge.

Battling against mere mortals no longer amused him. He began to believe that he was truly unbeatable, as the legends about him told. He needed a new enemy to vanquish, new lands to conquer, and new adventures to feed his wanderlust. He sought excitement.

He was not disappointed.

A stranger washed up on the shores of the island that would later become the emerald city of Magnapor. Barely alive when discovered, the man whose name was lost to time, much like Kai's birth name, told a tale so tall that at first no one believed it.

No one save the man looking for new worlds to conquer.

Gengis Kai believed.

Hanging on the stranger's every word, the adventurer's heart beat faster with each new added detail. The newcomer told stories of a mysterious chain of islands nearby where the sailing ship upon which he served crashed.

The islands did not appear on any of the maps in the possession of his captain. They were large, craggy spindles growing up from beneath the ocean. Barely inhabitable by man, these islands were home to all manner of creature, bizarre beasts both large and small.

These creatures populated the island, but they did not rule it.

The islands were ruled by the Warriors of Hades.

It was Gengis Kai himself who hung the label on these fabled rulers who he described as massive human-like creatures with dark, flaming skin burning beneath rock-like shells. Everything they touched burned like lava.

Many scoffed at the lone survivor's fantastic story, laughing at the absurdity of it, but not their monarch. Gengis Kai listened with rapt attention, taking in every detail as the man spoke, weaving a tale that grew more outlandish as it continued.

"Surely, sire, you do not believe this man's lies?" one of his trusted aides asked when he had a moment alone with the Kai.

"Have we not seen great beasts on the open sea, my brother?" Kai said, his voice rising so all could hear. "Have we not overcome obstacles that no mere mortal men could have faced and survived? Have we not met the enemy in all its forms? Tall, short, wide, size matters not. Have we not witnessed things in our travels, my friends, things that would make lesser men shudder and soil themselves?"

Gengis Kai's followers nodded, muttered agreements.

"Have we not discovered things that were merely myth until we held them in our hands?"

"YES!"

"And have we not feasted on the sweetest meat torn from great beasts the likes of which have never before been seen?"

"YES!"

"Then why, my friends… why do you doubt our new friend's tale? Why is his adventure not as believable as our own?"

"Yeah!"

"I tell you, my brothers and sisters, if I thought that those who were told of our exploits did not believe them, I would take proper offense. Would you do any less?"

"No!"

"Then why do you disrespect our honored guest so?"

The room fell quiet. Many of Kai's followers stared at their feet, embarrassed and properly chastised.

"I say we continue the festivities tonight for tomorrow we set sail!"

The crowd erupted in a roar.

"Adventure awaits, my friends," Gengis Kai said, smiling. "Who are we to disappoint adventure?"

The crowd cheered as the party blossomed into a full-blown celebration. A new adventure was on the horizon and Gengis Kai was the king of adventure. He was ready to once again face the unknown.

Leaving the islands in the hands of trusted lieutenants who would not try to steal his lands for themselves, Gengis Kai sailed off into the unknown at day break, with only the wind at his back and the strength of his indomitable will to spurn him onward.

His new companion, the sold survivor of a doomed expedition, stood nervously at his side. He would serve as guide and, if it turned out that his stories were works of fiction as opposed to a great truth, he would also serve as an example to anyone who even dared to lie to the mighty Gengis Kai.

Legend tells that Gengis Kai did find the island and faced off against the rock lava creatures who dwelled there and defeated them.

The story of Gengis Kai and the Warriors of Hades was passed down from generation to generation. Even as the volcano erupted all around him, Gengis Kai fought the rock lava creatures until there was nothing left of the island and the sea reclaimed it.

Gengis Kai was gone.

"Wow," Buck Tellonger said, interrupting Simon Prentiss' story. "What happened to this Kai guy? Did he make it off the island?"

Simon Prentiss smiled. He knew he had the pilot's attention.

"Many wondered if Gengis Kai escaped the island," Mr. Tellonger. If so, where did he go? That is a question that has been posed by many. Still others believed that Gengis Kai still fights the Warriors of Hades in their home realm, keeping them trapped there for all eternity and away from the Earth, which Gengis Kai still believes belongs to him."

"That's amazing," Buck said as he stubbed out his nub of a cigar and popped another into his mouth. Thankfully, the Great and Powerful not only allowed smoking, but also encouraged it. The smoke added to the club's appeal. "Which version of the story do you buy?"

"Here it comes," Lance muttered.

"I believe that Gengis Kai survived the destruction of the mysterious island. Instead of returning to the life he had known, I believe he set aside the mantle and costume of Gengis Kai and roamed the earth, working in service to those he once enslaved."

"Why would he do that?" Buck asked.

"No one knows for certain, and I can feel lance rolling his eyes as I say it, but I think the eruption of the volcano changed him. Maybe he experienced a vision like Saul in the Bible before he changed his name to Paul and dedicated his life to a new, worthy cause."

"You think the volcano was Gengis Kai's version of a burning bush?" Lance asked.

"Why not? It's as plausible as anything else."

"It's just a story, Simon," Lance said, a little louder than he intended. "There is absolutely no evidence that this Gengis Kai existed. You're still just chasing shadows like you always have."

"Not anymore, Lance."

Simon leaned in a bit closer to his friend, his annoyance showing through. He stabbed the table with a finger to emphasize his point.

"You never were a true believer were you, Lance? Not like your father. He understood the importance of the crown. He understood. Your father was a true believer."

"You leave dad out of this!" Lance shouted, angry. He pointed an accusing finger at Simon, the threat clear.

"You know as well as I do that Landon Star would have dropped everything to help me recover this treasure!"

"I'm warning you, Simon—" Lance said, pushing away from the table.

Lance walked away in the direction of the bar's bathroom.

"Dammit," Simon muttered, a fist bouncing off the table. "I thought I had him this time."

"I take it this is not a new argument," Buck said.

"No. This is an old, old fight," Prentiss said. "One I doubt we'll ever finish."

"I don't know about that," Buck said as he lit the cigar.

"You heard the man. He doesn't believe me."

"Maybe not, but there's one thing you need to consider," Buck said as he blew a thick cloud of smoke around a friendly smile.

"And what's that?"

"Whether he believes you or not," Buck said. "Lance Star just flew halfway around the world to help you. That's got to say something, don't it?"

Now it was Simon Prentiss' turn to smile.

"I like the way you think, Buck."

"Smart chaps like yourself usually do," Buck joked.

4.

Lance was still steamed as he walked back to the table.

And another thing," Lance started as he sat back down. He still had plenty of fight left in him, but didn't want to have this particular battle with Simon yet again. Not today. It was an old argument, one that he knew would never be solved until either he or Simon gave in, even if just a little.

They were both equally stubborn men.

Sadly, that meant neither of them planned to give an inch and the disagreement continued.

Noting his friend's rising ire, and not wanting to see two old friends start throwing punches, Buck Tellonger intervened by pouring each of them a fresh glass.

"Ease off, mates," Buck said as he handed each man their drink. "Professor Prentiss, we just traveled halfway around the world to meet with you. That should tell you just how good a friend you have here. And Lance, you wouldn't have come if you didn't want to help your friend, would you?"

The air ace shook his head.

"You're right, of course, Mr. Tellonger," Prentiss said. "I'm sorry, Lance. Forgive me for picking an old fight?"

"It's okay," Lance said after taking a sip of his beer. "No hard feelings?"

"None whatsoever."

Lance and Simon shook hands as a smiling Buck looked on.

"It's just… I've never been so close before, Lance," Prentiss said, his excitement palpable. "The crown is on this island. I know it. I feel it."

"Why here?"

"Magnapor was one of the islands that Gengis Kai was rumored to have conquered during his conflict with the Warriors of Hades. The stories of his exploits say that the Kai exiled the monsters to the burning cauldron from whence they sprung."

"These would be the rocky lava guys?" Lance said.

"Yes. I know how silly it sounds, Lance. Believe me, I do, but aren't you the one who told me about flying into an alternate universe once or the time you fought Nazi's riding pterodactyl's? How is this any less believable than that?"

"He's got you there, boss," Buck said, unable to stifle a snicker.

With a sigh, Lance surrendered to the inevitable. He had never been able to say no to his friends and Simon was no exception. Buck was right. Lance already knew he was going to help his friend the minute he set a course for Magnapor island.

"Okay," Lance said, holding up his arms in surrender. "You've convinced me. I'm in."

"That's great! Now, the first thing we need to do is…" Simon started, but Lance silenced his friend with a gesture to calm down.

"Not so fast, Simon. he first thing we have to do is shake our friends over there."

"Friends?" Simon asked, confused. He started to turn away from the conversation and look for whoever Lance was talking about, but his friend grabbed his arm to keep him from moving.

"Take it easy," Lance said. "You got 'em, Buck?"

"Yeah. I clocked them earlier. They followed us in and have been trying hard not to stare at us ever since they sat down."

"What friends?" Simon asked again. "What're you talking about?"

"We picked up a tail. Somebody is following us... probably to get to you."

"Why would anyone be worried about me?" Simon asked. "I'm nothing special. No one would pay a ransom for me. Not even my family. Who would be interested in me?"

"They would," Lance said, nodding easily toward the table where the two agents sat. "Look, but don't be obvious, okay?"

"Right," Simon said and tried to play it casual, but a secret agent he was not. He peered through the smokey haze until he saw the two men Lance had pointed out and his eyes went wide.

"They've been tailing us since we left the airfield," Buck added. "Any idea who they are?"

"Yes," Simon said softly. "They're The Overlord's men.

"Those guys work for this Overlord of yours?"

"I'm afraid so. They're part of his not-so-secret police force. I'd recognize his goons anywhere. Subtle they are not."

"Remember what I told you," Buck said. "On this island, The Overlord is the Big Kahuna, Lance. You don't make a move on Magnapor without it getting back to him and if you step out of line, he sics the goon squad on you."

"Please tell me you cleared your little treasure hunt with the local government before you started poking around in their back yard," Lance asked Simon.

"Not exactly."

"What does that mean, not exactly?" Lance asked, once again growing annoyed.

"The Overlord is not what you'd call a nice guy," Simon started.

"Really? Did you expect a guy who calls himself *The Overlord* to be a sweetheart of a guy?"

"No, and that's why I have been trying to, how it you say, fly below the radar."

"And a good job you're doing of it too, Simon," Lance said.

"But I…"

Before Professor Prentiss could say more, Lance noticed a third man join the two agents at their table. The odds were now one to one, but hardly even. Island security was stringent. After landing, Lance and Buck had both been searched. The only weapons they had were still on the plane. They were unarmed.

Lance doubted the same could be said for The Overlord's secret police officers.

"We cannot let The Overlord get his hands on the crown. With it his reach could exceed beyond this island. It would make him even more dangerous."

"Easy now, mate," Buck said, trying to calm Simon down before he drew even more attention toward their small table. "Professor, you make it sound like this crown of yours has bloody magical powers or something."

"Not exactly, Buck. However, As a symbol it is very powerful indeed, one that the natives will understand. With the crown of Gengis Kai in his possession, The Overlord could--"

"Better table that for now, Simon," Lance said. Looks like your friends are on the move."

Sure enough, Agents Smith and Jones got to their feet, accompanied by the new arrival, Agent White. Although none of the men they approached knew they names, which were no doubt aliases, Lance and Buck had dealt with their kind before.

Both Lance and Buck hated bullies and that's what men like The Overlord and those who worked for him were… bullies. Landon Star had taught his son that the best way to deal with bullies was to give as good as they gave. A bully's best weapon was intimidation. Lance's father taught him to stand against such tactics and most of the time, the bully would back down. On those rare occasions when the bad guy stood his ground, Landon instructed his son to do the same. He also taught him how to throw a punch.

Lance Star had been standing up to bullies all his life.

These three men and their boss were nothing special.

"Buck?"

"It's covered, boss," Buck said.

The three of them got to their feet, but made no attempt to run. So far, The Overlord's agents kept their weapons holstered. Lance wanted to keep it that way. The last thing he wanted was for them to start shooting wild inside the crowded club.

Smiling, Buck stood and cupped a hand over his cigar as if to light it. He still held his beer. He looked more like a drunk than a threat.

The agents got closer.

"Buck?"

"Hang tight, Lance," Buck mumbled around the cigar between his lips.

Agents Smith and Jones stopped in front of Buck, who was paying them no attention.

"Our employer wishes to speak with you," Agent Jones said with authority. "He has questions for you."

"You will come with us," Agent Smith added.

"One of you chaps wouldn't happen to have a light, would you?" Buck asked, still smiling and fumbling with his cigarette lighter.

"Stand aside," Agent Smith said as he pushed past Buck.

"What the!" Buck started.

Buck stumbled, which caused him to spill his beer.

"Hey!" he shouted.

As if in a comedic play, Buck sent the sudsy brew flying with flourish. He managed to keep hold of the cigar in his teeth, but the beer splattered everywhere.

"Get out of the way, you bumbling fool!" Agent Jones shouted.

Seething, Buck Tellonger looked from the beer staining his shirt to the three men standing in front of him. His teeth tightened on the cigar clenched there until he almost bit it clean in two. A growl rose up from deep inside the bulldog of a man. Buck Tellonger was shorter than the agents by a few inches, but he was built like a linebacker and had the temper of an angry grizzly bear. Most people underestimated the pilot because he played the comic relief so often compared to Lance Star's more serious tone. It was a dynamic that worked for them, especially in situations like the one they now found themselves in.

It was surprising to Lance how often these situations cropped up.

Before the agents could issue another command, Buck's expression shifted from rage to something far more sinister. He smiled and his handlebar mustache rose comically as he showed teeth around his smelly five cent cigar.

With spilled beer on his shirt, Buck looked at the three men a, still smiling and ready to throw down if they gave him provocation. Spilling his beer fit the bill.

Buck loved a good bar fight.

"Oh, mate, you've gone and done it now," he said. "This was my favorite shirt. My mother bought me this shirt for Christmas last year."

"I don't care," Agent Smith said and tried to move Buck aside with a slight push.

Buck pushed back.

"Where I come from, we mind our manners, sonny," Buck said.

With a growl, the bulky air ace laid into the men, tossing a haymaker that knocked one of the agents off his feet and the other slammed into a nearby table, sending its contents crashing to the floor along with the agent and the table. He dropped to the hardwood floor with a loud **THUD!**

The other agent reacted quickly and moved toward the belligerent drunk.

The agents no longer seemed concerned about Lance Star or Simon Prentiss, which had been Buck's intention all along. He would keep the agents busy while Lance got his professor friend out of there safely.

"Come on," Lance said. "Is there a side door out of this place?"

"Yes," Simon said, pointing. "That way."

"Good. Let's get you out of here."

"What about your friend? Is he going to be okay?"

"Are you kidding? He's having the time of his life," Lance said, smiling as he cast a last look back into the bar where Buck was working his magic before walking through the door.

Lance knew that the air ace could handle himself. Buck Tellonger had been scrapping for over twenty years and was a veteran of two big wars and a lot of smaller skirmishes. Just a week earlier, they had been in a dogfight with Japanese Zeroes near Espritos Marcos in the Pacific. He could handle himself in a fight.

Lance couldn't say the same about Simon Prentiss. Simon had spent the last several years with his nose in a book, trying to find his missing treasure. He hadn't met too many archaeology professors who could handle themselves in a fight. Except that one guy he met in Egypt. He had been able to protect himself well enough.

Buck threw a hard left into the jaw of Agent Jones.

The agent staggered, but somehow remained on his feet.

Before Buck could finish him off, Agent White came around to flank him.

Buck had seen similar maneuvers before. The Overlord's men were not well trained when it came to hand-to-hand combat. Not surprising. They were used to dealing with locals most of the time and the people who called Magnapor home had been conditioned to fear the agents.

This was not a problem for Buck Tellonger.

Grabbing Agent White by the jacket collar, Buck pulled him in close instead of throwing a punch like the man expected. Off balance, he pitched forward into Buck's waiting knee, which connected with the agent's midsection, doubling him over.

Buck threw him to the floor.

"Who's next?" Buck shouted.

Agents Smith and Jones were back on their feet and circled the pilot.

"You are under arrest," Agent Smith shouted. "You and your friends!"

"What friends?"

The agents had been so busy squaring off against the man they thought was a belligerent drunk that they hadn't noticed the other two men sneaking away.

They had escaped.

"Where did they go?" Agent White shouted.

"Tell us where your friends went to or…" Agent Jones started, turning back to face their opponent.

That's when they realized that the man with the handlebar mustache was also gone.

"How did…? Agent Smith shouted.

The agents looked around the room, but saw no sign of their quarry. The denizens of the Great and Powerful stared at them, all eyes on the three agents who had just had their hats handed to them. The Overlord's wrath was well known to the locals. Everyone in Magnapor understood that failure was not tolerated.

The agents had lost their targets.

None of them were eager to report their failure to The Overlord.

5.

The mountains of Magnapor Island glowed as the sun set behind them, painting the dusky sky in shades of oranges and reds that turned purple the higher you looked until the inky black of nightfall started down to meet the dark waters of the ocean waves.

The Overlord's tower glistened in the sun's final light like sparkling green emeralds reflecting firelight. Everyone in the Emerald City below would be able to see the beauty of the island's tallest structure. Surely, they would be in awe of its majesty, The Overlord thought of the peasants below.

To most, it was called The Spire.

To the man who lived in its uppermost levels, The Overlord simply called it home.

Like so many other dictators in various corners of the globe, The Overlord was not a man of the people. Those who served under his pleasure on the island feared him. He ruled the island with an iron fist. If you stayed on his good side and kicked back your cut to his agents on time and paid in full, then the island of Magnapor offered safe haven. If you stepped out of line, there was no place you could hide on the island.

Though there were thousands of locals who were native to the island, most of them farmers and day laborers, the vast majority of Magnapor's occupants were smugglers and thieves, ne'er do wells on the run from either the law or someone out to do them harm. The Overlord welcomed them all. They were his kind of people.

As the world fell apart around them, Magnapor stood apart from the warring nations whose squabbling and posturing threatened to plunge the world once more into a world-wide war. When nations unleashed their fury upon one another, small island nations like Magnapor and Scavenger Quay, to name but a few, were often caught in the crossfire and destroyed.

The Overlord was working all of the angles to keep his powerbase safe. That meant recruiting men and women with certain skillsets that could be used to protect the island and perhaps even turn the tides of war if it came to that.

While recruitment continued, The Overlord had his best and brightest researching weaponry, offensive and defensive strategies, tactics, and even unconventional methods of protecting his island in the event of an all-out conflict.

When word reached him that a world-renowned archaeologist named Simon Prentiss had come to his island unannounced, The Overlord became intrigued. The research his team dug up on the man showed him to be an expert on a dangerous artifact worn by a hero of legend. Even The Overlord had heard the stories about the legendary Gengis Kai, a man who folklore claims tamed a string off islands throughout the Pacific and the South China Sea, including the volcano The Overlord now called home—Magnapor.

Like anyone who had spent any amount of time in the region, whether born there or migrated, The Overlord had heard the story of Gengis Kai and the Warriors of Hades before. The legend had been passed down from generation to generation with Kai's prowess growing with each new retelling. Many versions ended with the heroic Kai dying in a volcanic eruption to keep the Warriors of Hades trapped beneath the mantle. Gengis Kai fought these creatures from myth until there was nothing left of the island and the sea reclaimed it.

Lucky for The Overlord, the destruction of the island had not set well with the sea so it had to spit the island back onto to the surface in time for him to claim it as his own.

It was all superstitious nonsense, of course, but there was one thing all of the stories of the great Gengis Kai had in common.

He was powerful.

The Overlord wanted that power. If there was even the slimmest of chances that Professor Prentiss could find it, The Overlord wanted to make certain he had it. He assigned a cadre of hand-picked agents to tail the scientist and learn all they could about his work and, if all went well, they could follow him to the crown.

So far, the professor had been a disappointment.

Until today.

"Are you certain of the facts?"

The Overlord stood tall, easily six foot four with wide shoulders and a fighter's physique. In his mid to late 40's, he was moderately handsome, with a full head of jet-black hair that hung past his collar before the ends started to curl back upward. His short cropped black mustache and goatee covered a sharp chin.

The Overlord stood at the far edge of the room, flipping through several file folders filled with reports from various agents around the island. A man in his position had to keep on top of the goings on around him lest the riff raff, as he saw them, who lived below, got out of hand. The only reason he hadn't run every last single one of them off of his island was because he needed them. The Overlord's wealth was built on the backs of those who served him. He would never admit it aloud, but he needed the worked of Magnapor more than they needed him.

He dreaded the day they realized this to be true.

On that day, his great dream of a stunning emerald city would truly die.

And him right along with it.

Wearing a very expensive tailor-made suit and jacket, The Overlord stood before one of the floor to ceiling windows that filled two walls of his opulent office. The space looked more like a study that a working office. One of the advantages of being rich and owning the building was that you got to decorate your own way. The Overlord was a collector of rare items himself. Shelves along the walls were filled with statuary, baubles, paintings, and assorted treasures that he had picked up in his travels. He was rather fond of ancient antiquities.

"Yes, sir," Agent Sunday said, nervous. Depending on the man's mood, The Overlord was known to react badly to unhappy news.

The report Agent Sunday had handed over did not contain any positive news.

"The report is accurate."

Closing the file, The Overlord tossed the stack of them onto his desk before turning to face his agent across the desk that separated them. A photo slid out of the folder on top.

"Are you certain of the newcomer's identity, Agent Sunday?"

"I am, Your Excellence. I have a surveillance team watching them as we speak."

"Well done."

"Thank you, sir."

The Overlord stepped to the desk and slammed his knuckles into it, bending the photo that had slipped free of the file folder. It was a grainy photo of a blonde man with a big, bright smile. Agent Sunday recognized him as the man his squadron was following.

"What do you know of this man?" The Overlord asked.

"His name is Lance Star. He is a celebrity pilot from the United States. He signs autographs and flies stunt shows for his adoring fans."

"So, you do believe him to be a threat?"

"I would not dismiss him so easily, sir. Although he is no longer a member of the United States Armed Forces, Lance Star flew numerous combat missions during the last war. It is also rumored that he still flies missions against the Axis for the US War Department as a reservist along with his squadron of reserve pilots. They call themselves the Sky Rangers."

"That name rings a bell," The Overlord said, rubbing a finger and thumb though his beard.

"You probably saw them in a newsreel," Agent Sunday said. "The world news loves to follow their exploits. Last year, he foiled a sabotage scheme in his own New York. They also disrupted a scheme by German scientists to weaponize indigenous wildlife in the Ring of Fire to use in an attack against the southern United States."

"I remember hearing something about that. There was a volcano, if I remember correctly."

"That's correct, sir. The island was all but destroyed in the ensuing eruption. Star and his confederates barely had time to escape in time."

"But they did escape?"

"Yes, sir."

"And now he's here on my island."

"Yes, sir."

"Do we know why this famous American pilot would come here? Why did he come to my city?"

"No, sir. I do not know for certain. However, after securing his plane at the airport, Lance Star hailed a cab. Upon his arrival in the city, Mr. Star and his companion, a man we have identified as Buck Tellonger, also an air ace circa World War One and a member of the Sky Rangers, met with the treasure hunter, Simon Prentiss at a bar."

"Prentiss?" The Overlord repeated, almost spitting the word.

"Yes, sir," Agent Sunday said, trying to keep his boss' ire from turning to anger that could be aimed his direction.

The Overlords hands balled into fists around the files on the desk, crumpling them. He knew the name Simon Prentiss all too well. He had been suspicious of the man after his agents reported that the noted archaeology professor had come to their shores. The Overlord was not a fan of anyone who came to his island thinking they could dig up an old treasure and carry it home with them.

If there really was treasure hidden on Magnapor, The Overlord would be the one to keep it for himself. He would rather see it remain hidden before letting a stranger deliver it to some museum. He sighed.

"I should have killed that man when I had the chance," he said through grit teeth.

Agent Sunday started to comment, but thought better of it and remained silent. Nothing he could say or do would calm the man's anger.

Like the flip of a switch, The Overlord's mood changed. He stood straight, flexed his fingers, then turned back to stare out at the beautiful Emerald City stretched out below. Standing in front of the floor to ceiling window, hands clasped behind his back, The Overlord stared at his city, his island, and the volcano in the distance.

"Do you know where they are now?"

"Yes, sir," Agent Sunday said. "I have three agents at the Great and Powerful Bar. The agents are under orders to keep all three of them there, forcibly if necessary."

"Bring them to me."

"Yes, sir."

Agent Sunday bowed and left the office as quickly as he could. Before he became an agent of The Overlord's secret police, the man who would become Agent Sunday was a warrior himself. Like Lance Star and many others in his command, Sunday had been boots on the ground during the waning days of the Word War, which they called the war to end all wars. He had seen more than his fair share of bloody engagements. He had killed men in battle, watched them die through the sights of his rifle and close up on those occasions when he used nothing more than his bare hands.

War did not scare Agent Sunday.

However, this buried treasure that the professor claimed to be searching for, the mythical Crown of Gengis Kai, terrified him deep into his bones. As he hurried to carry out his order and bring Simon Prentiss and his American pilot friends to The Overlord, Agent Sunday couldn't decide if he wanted to find the treasure or not.

Whatever happened next, Agent Sunday knew there would be bloodshed.

He only hoped the emerald city was not awash in it come the morning.

6.

Buck Tellonger was all smiles when he stepped into the alley.

He couldn't remember the last time he had been in a dust up like the bar fight inside *The Great and Powerful* club. The three goons in their trench coats and their stormtrooper tactics put forth an intimidating look, but Buck had been fighting the good fight for years, possibly longer than some of the men he had put down.

It wasn't that he loved violence. Buck preferred to calm tensions with a good joke and a round of beers, but not all situations worked out that way. His run in with The Overlord's men was one such encounter.

A part of him wished he could have stuck around long enough to right and fully trounce his opponents, but Buck was a tactician. Every move he made was deliberate, unless he'd had one too many at the local pub. Then, he could be a bit careless, but never ever on the job.

All he had to do was keep the agents busy long enough for Lance and his friend, Simon Prentiss to slink away unnoticed. Once they made their way out of the line of fire, Buck started planning his escape as well. Those who opposed him were often left surprised. Buck was a short, bulldog of a man who always seemed to be in need of a haircut and a shave. Not that he would ever consider losing the handlebar mustache. He was convinced that women loved the look, especially on a war hero pilot such as himself. To an outsider, he did not appear to be much of a threat. When the fight was over, Buck had happily schooled them on the truth. He was a scrapper with fists that hit like a sledgehammer.

A lesson the agents following them had learned all too well.

Getting away from the agents was the easy part. They might have worked as official state police for their boss, The Overlord, but it didn't take Buck long to size them up. They were bullies. They weren't trained. When dealing with the locals, the idea of the agents was probably enough to end whatever trouble had started. The Overlord ruled by fear and they relied on the despot's ruthless reputation to keep the natives in line.

Once he had the agents off kilter, which wasn't that hard, truth be told, Buck ducked into the kitchen instead of heading toward the club's front door. Only a fool would think that escape was possible through that crowd. The kitchen was crowded, but unguarded. The club's security was focused on the front entrance and the areas occupied by customers, not their employees.

Buck used that to his advantage.

Minutes later, the air ace pushed his way through the alley door to freedom.

The first thing he noticed was the stench. Against the wall stood two dumpsters. Two additional dumpsters sat at the far end of the alley as well, each set used by different businesses. Buck vaguely recalled a restaurant in the building that shared the alley with The Great and Powerful. The smell told him he was in the right place, but Buck tried not to get ahead of himself.

One of the tenets of growing older is that wisdom accompanies age.

When he was younger, Buck Tellonger had the unfortunate habit of leaping without looking. This had a tendency to lead the young man astray. He often found himself in some rather hot water more times than he cared to admit. Even his parents, God rest their souls, had all but given up on him. His father had once told Buck that he "*would be lucky to reach thirty.*"

Buck couldn't disagree.

After enlisting, he was all but certain his lifespan would be short.

His reckless abandon was an asset as well as a curse. Buck turned out to be one hell of a soldier and he came home from the war with a box full of medals and twice as many disciplinary reports. He knew how to fight the enemy and he took it to the mat every time. The problem was, Buck didn't know who his friends were. To him, everyone was the enemy.

Then he met a gangly American pilot named Lance Star.

Lance did not stand for Buck's reckless behavior. They clashed a few times in those early days, but eventually the two became friends. Fighting side by side against the enemy only served to strengthen that bond and when Lance Star returned to the states at the end of the war to start up his own aviation manufacture business, he asked Buck to join him on a new adventure.

To his own surprise, Buck said yes.

Years later, Lance would tell Buck that he considered the older pilot a mentor. Buck also thought the same of his friend, though his pride rarely allowed him to speak the words out loud.

Working with Lance and the other Sky Rangers was one adventure after the other and he was having the time of his life. Since joining up with his friend, Buck had seen more of the world than he ever believed possible. Many cases, they managed to visit exotic locales without getting shot at, though that wasn't always the case. The Sky Rangers had made many an enemy in their time and danger was just as much a part of their charter as action and adventure.

The alley was clear, save for heaps of trash scattered about. Once he was sure there was no need to duck back inside The Great and Powerful's kitchen,

Buck allowed the door to close and latch behind him, automatically locking when closed.

"Okay, where are ya, Lance?" he muttered.

The alley was open at both ends. To the left was another restaurant. To the right was a highway. Both ways could be used to circle back around to the front of the club.

Or from the club, Buck realized when one of the agents stepped around the corner to the right.

Their eyes locked.

Before the agent could sound the alarm and alert his companions to their target's whereabouts, Buck bit back an expletive. The fight had simply paused and changed venue. The agents were more resourceful than he had first expected.

Buck bolted toward the left side of the alley as fast as he could, leaving the agent shouting after him. Without looking back, Buck ran as fast as he could, hearing the agent's shoes slap the asphalt behind him. The pilot was beginning to regret that last pitcher of beer.

At the entrance to the alley, he slowed long enough to make sure there were no surprises waiting for him around the corner of the building.

The coast was clear.

Buck ducked around the corner then stopped.

Like the other streets he had seen in Magnapor's major city, the sidewalks were filled with vendors and hucksters hawking their goods and services on the populace. The streets were over-crowded, which made it difficult to get anywhere in a hurry, but it was great if you needed to disappear into the crowd.

Buck wasn't a man prone to running. Walking away from a fight rankled his sensibilities, but the air ace also understood that sometimes the mission, which is what their little trek to an island paradise, was turning into.

Whatever Simon Prentiss had gotten himself into was obviously worse than he let on. Surely the secret police had not been sic'd on him because of an ancient legend about a magical crown worn by a man who fought lava monsters. Surely, there had to be something else. Simon had to have uncovered something else, some long-buried secret that could hurt The Overlord.

"Damned legends," Buck muttered as his gave fell upon a small broken pallet leaning against the wall. It had once held one of the many street vendor's wares.

Now, it was a weapon.

Buck snapped off a board from the pallet and hefted it easily. The wood was hard, thick enough to survive on a cargo ship at sea. It was more than up to the task the pilot had in mind for it. His back against the brick wall, Buck settled into his best baseball stance.

He held his breath and listened as the footfalls got closer.

Closer.

Buck swung for the bleachers.

The flat piece of timber caught the agent in the gut, bending him forward at the midsection in a fit of pain. The agent held his stomach even as he crumpled to the pavement.

"One down."

Buck pulled the man back into the alley and sat him next to the dumpster. He was out light a light, but Buck decided it was best to stash him out of sight if anyone from the street looked into the alley. The longer his friend stayed out of sight, the better it was for Buck and his friends. He pulled the belt from the trench coat and used it to tie the unconscious agent's arms behind his back.

Moments later, now wearing the agent's fedora, Buck stepped out of the alley.

He turned left and blended into the crowd.

###

Buck stuck to the plan.

After a few disastrous visits to strange lands, like Magnapor, the Sky Rangers had developed a sure-fire system in case they ran into local trouble and had to split up. Usually, the best course of action was to head back to the plane they arrived in. That way, whoever arrived first could protect the aircraft and secure their flight back home.

It was a tried and true strategy.

There were times when adjustments were required. This struck him as one of those occasions. Buck knew that Lance was intent on helping his friend, Simon. Escape wasn't at the top of the professor's *to do* list, however. No matter what else hc knew about Simon Prentiss, Buck recognized the man's single-minded pursuit of the Crown of Gengis Kai. Finding the crown was why he had called Lance and asked him to fly to Magnapor.

There was no way he would leave without finishing what he started.

That meant Lance would not make a beeline for the plane after escaping the ambush at the club. Instead, Lance would head to wherever Simon had been staying or working so they could collect his research. From there, they would seek out the crown and try to retrieve it before escaping the island.

Unfortunately, for Buck, he had no idea where Professor Prentiss lived or worked. In fact, he had no idea where to start looking for the hidden treasure they sought. Simon had kept the details private, even from his friend who had flown halfway around the world to help him.

Simon was an archaeologist, but Buck also sensed that he was true believer. The crown's historical significance was valuable, but if you believed the stories that the crown bestowed untold power onto the person who wore it atop their head, it was priceless.

If you believed in that sort of mumbo-jumbo.

Buck wasn't sure what he believed.

All he knew was that he needed to find Lance and soon.

By the time he reached the outer fence of the airfield, he could clearly see that the hangar they had rented was dark and apparently undisturbed. There was no sign of Lance either. That all but proved his theory.

Three options were open to him and Buck wasn't sure which was the best course to pursue. He could wait until Lance and Simon showed up and hope all was well. That option did not sound appealing at all. He could call in reinforcements and hope the Sky Rangers would arrive in time. The flight time all but guaranteed that their friends wouldn't be able to reach them in time. The last option was to head back into town and look for Lance and his friend.

None of the options were exceptionally helpful, but Buck wasn't prone to waiting around. He hoped the fence and headed toward the hangar. If Lance had stopped there first, he would have left word on their next move. If not, Buck would help himself to the weapons stored in the plane's hidden compartments.

Either way, Buck would be on the move soon.

"Hang on, boys," the air ace said as he slipped a handgun into his belt. "Your wingman's on his way.

7.

Lance Star found an out of the way corner and ducked inside.

The smart course of action was to keep moving. The Overlord's men were no doubt dogging their trail. The only way to stay safe was to keep moving. Unfortunately, Lance's passenger was slowing things down. Simon Prentiss was a professor and archaeologist. He was used to slow, intricate dats spent focused on studies or a swath of earth.

Running for his life while being hunted by a tiny island nation's secret police was a little outside his field of expertise. The man had already started to struggle for breath before they made it out of the alley. Now, his breathing was labored, heavy, so much so that Lance had begun to fear his friend might have a heart attack.

Lance pulled Simon into the tiny alcove at the edge of the Emerald City's bazaar, one of the largest outdoor markets in the entire South Pacific.

As soon as Buck Tellonger had tossed the agent to the floor, all eyes were on him. Lance seized the opportunity his friend had created and promptly pushed Simon Prentiss toward the kitchen. On the outside, Buck might look like a schlub, thanks to his unkempt nature, mussed hair, and thick mangled cigar clutched in his teeth, but he was a bulldog in a fight. Dangerous, quick to anger, and tenacious. He wouldn't stop brawling until his opponents were on the floor or he was and that was something you could take to the bank.

Lance knew the old warhorse could take care of himself, even with the three to one odds.

Simon Prentiss, on the other hand, had never been in a fistfight his entire life, which seemed odd considering how often Lance himself had found himself in a scrap or twelve since they were almost always together growing up.

Simon was a natural born scholar. He looked at the world like a giant jigsaw puzzle that needed to be solved where all of the pieces were supposed to fit together perfectly to form a fully realized whole.

That was not the world Lance Star lived in.

As a man who had been involved in two wars and more battles than he cared to count, Lance held a more cynical view of the world. He knew there were evil men out there whose sole purpose was to watch the world burn. There was no rhyme or reason to it. The planet was large enough for everyone, but for some of the would-be tyrants he and the Sky Rangers had taken down, the world was not enough. They wanted to either rule it all or watch it go up in cinders.

As long as those people existed, Lance Star and his team would stand up and fight., before…

Lance looked around. They blended in with the thick crowd congregating in the bazaar, but it wasn't safe to stay in one place too long. If the word hadn't gone out about them, no doubt with accompanying photographs, it wouldn't be long before they started circulating them. Lance had to get them out of the city fast before…

That's when he saw it and realized it was too late.

Lance's gaze drew skyward when he heard a loud horn sound. It reminded him of the air raid alerts back home, though not quite as urgent. On the side of the tallest buildings, the ones controlled by The Overlord, were projection screens. The best Lance could tell was that projectors inside the building pushed the image outward so it could be seen from the street. There was no sound, but the pictures told the story.

Images of a bar fight danced across the large screens. With no sound they could not hear the report, but a man in a tailored suit read from a sheet of yellow paper while photographs of Lance Star, Buck Tellonger, and Simon Prentiss floated behind him with their names emblazoned beneath each image. On an empty corner of the screen was information stating that these men were being sought for questioning by Island Police and a call for Magnapor's citizens to report any sightings of these dangerous men to their local authorities as quickly as possible.

The message ended with *Your cooperation will be rewarded* in white on a field of black.

Seconds later, the news report repeated.

"Simon, we've got to get moving," he told his friend. "It won't take them long to find us now. We've got to go!"

"How are you not out of breath?"

"Clean living," Lance said with a chuckle.

He offered a hand.

"I gave up cigarettes and got back into the routine of a daily run like we used to do back in the service. You'd be amazed how much it helps."

"You run on purpose?"

"Of course."

"You ever see me running, there's probably something chasing me," Simon said as his friend helped him back to his feet.

Lance laughed.

"So, where to?" Simon asked.

"The way I see it, we've got two choices. We can make a break for the airfield and get the hell off this island."

"Or?"

"Or we go find this treasure of yours so we'll have some leverage against The Overlord and then we get the hell off this island."

"I vote plan B."

"I thought you might," Lance said. "Where to?"

"It's on the other side of the island."

"Of course it is," Lance muttered. "Okay, the hangar it is then."

"No. We have to go back to my hotel."

"Bad idea, Simon. If there's one place we can expect to find the bad guys, it's at your hotel."

"You don't understand," Simon said as they moved deeper into the crowd. "All of my research is there. I need it."

"Of course you do."

"Lance, please!"

"If they haven't torn your room apart yet, they will soon. What are the odds we get there and collect your notes before they do?"

"Pretty good, actually."

"How so?"

Simon smiled. "I hid them."

This brought the pilot up short.

"You hid them?"

"Of course," Simon said, still smiling. "I'm not a complete idiot, you know."

"I guess not. Okay, so where are they?"

"I hid a waterproof bag behind the fountain in the lobby," Simon said, proud of himself.

Lance stopped and stared at his friend. "This is one of the poorest places on Earth, but your hotel has a lobby fountain? Where exactly are you staying, Simon?"

Simon pointed to the tall green building that sat next door to the tall green skyscraper where The Overlord lived.

"Oh, that's just great," Lance said.

"And you're sure you can't find this crown of yours without that research?"

"Positive."

"Okay. Come on," Lance said, changing course and heading straight toward the lion's den. "Let me state, for the record, that I think this is a horrible idea."

"Noted."

Lance Star sighed and pushed forward, disappearing into the crowd.

###

Buck Tellonger's patience had neared its end.

He had been waiting what felt like forever for Lance and his professor friend to show up at the airfield. He had exited the club well after they had so there was no good reason for them not to have made it back before he did.

There were plenty of bad reasons though and each one of them danced around inside his brain. The most likely scenario was that had gotten caught by The Overlord's thugs. Lance could take care of himself, Buck knew, but even the best scraper could go down when the odds were stacked against them.

The Overlord definitely had more men at his disposal than the three of them could easily take on. Not that Buck wouldn't mind trying. He liked a good fight as much as the next man.

Speaking of The Overlord's thugs...

Buck ducked back beneath cover when the headlights from a car pulled into the airfield. The car made a beeline for the hangar he and Lance had rented for their stay. Another car pulled in only seconds behind the first and also parked near the hangar.

Well, this can't be good, he thought as he watched the four men huddle together. Two got out of the first car. Two more exited the second. They were each dressed in the uniform of the island's secret police.

Uh oh. Guess our secret's out, Buck thought as he moved into a better position to spy on the agents outside the hangar.

When he heard the faint SNAP! Of a twig snap behind him, he knew he was in trouble.

Buck spun hard just in time to the see the business end of a slapper hurling toward him.

He tried to dodge, but it was too late.

The pilot slumped to the ground, dazed and off balance.

Blood poured from the gash on his forehead.

The second hit, this one to the back of the head.

Buck Tellonger collapsed, unconscious.

The two agents standing over him grabbed the air ace by the arms and dragged him across the grass to the airfield where they summarily dumped him next to one of the cars.

"Any sign of his friends?" Agent Sunday asked.

"No, sir."

"Too bad," Sunday said. "Get him in the car. He has an appointment with his fate. And The Overlord does not like to be kept waiting.

8.

"I don't like the look of this," Lance Star said.

The Emerald Grand Hotel wasn't the most heavily fortified place he had ever had to break into, but security was impressive nonetheless. The lobby was massive and sported a large open ceiling where large chandeliers hung below a mural of a crisp, blue sky dotted with tiny, pleasant clouds. Near the reservation and check in counter at the rear of the lobby was a rock wall with a waterfall that trickled over layers of rock to the large pool that stretched out into the middle of the lobby. Chairs and tables were arranged along the perimeter of the pool for guests to eat, talk, or do business in peaceful surroundings.

"This is where you chose to hide out?" Lance asked.

Simon Prentiss shrugged.

"We really need to teach you how to blend in," Lance told his clueless friend. "What's your room number?"

"Fourteen Oh One," Simon said while pointing off to the left. "The elevator is over there."

"Please tell me you have the room key on you?"

Simon shook his head. "I always leave it with the front desk. I have a tendency to get lost in my work and misplace things like keys. This way I'm never locked out of my room and I can collect my messages when I return."

"Terrific. Who else knows you're here?"

"No one. Not this time. I left word with the university that I was going on sabbatical. They've begun to frown on my trips in search of the crown."

"What a shock," Lance said. "Maybe you should take the hint. No one but you believes this bloody crown exists."

"I don't understand why this bothers you," Simon said. "All I have to do is ask for it and they'll give me the key."

"I…" Lance grunted, reigned in his annoyance. He understood why all of this was getting to him. Simon's earlier crack about Lance's father had cut deep.

Simon Prentiss had always been a little dense when it came to understanding the reality of how the world worked. This was not news to the ace pilot. They had grown up together. Their parents were friends who sometimes worked together. Landon Star was himself a pilot, a strong man whose ideals young Lance Star had grown up to admire. Landon was the kind of man that Lance hoped to measure up to. They were very close.

Simon Prentiss and his father were also quite similar to one another. Professor Simon Prentiss Sr. was also a seeker of lost treasures. Unlike his son, however, his pursuits were more selfish in nature. The elder Professor Prentiss looked for treasures he could sell and cash in on whereas his son donated the vast majority of his finds to universities and museums for a small finder's fee worth only a fraction of the items real value.

Landon Star often teamed up with the elder Professor Prentiss on his excursions. Both Lance and Simon would sit and listen to their father spin their tall tales of adventure, intrigue, dangers that followed them as they sought out the world's greatest treasures. Lance often assumed that the men exaggerated their stories, making them much more exciting in the eyes of their children.

Now that he was older and had faced his own share of adventures, Lance wondered how many of those old tall tales were actually true. He wished more than anything that his father was still alive so he could ask.

When Simon had mentioned the Crown of Gengis Kai, Lance of course remembered it. Their fathers had gone on many an excursion in search of that elusive treasure. Each time they thought they had a lead, they would head off with the promise of new stories when they returned.

Lance remembered the disappointment in his father's eyes each time they came home without the crown in their possession.

Eventually, they gave up.

It wasn't long after that Professor Prentiss passed away. A heart attack took him in his sleep. It was a peaceful end. Simon, of course, took it hard. In the days and weeks that followed, as he poured through his father's papers, thoughts of finding and recovering the Crown of Gengis Kai consumed Simon Prentiss Jr. as it had his father.

In an effort to help his friend's son put his demons to rest, Landon Star agreed to rejoin the search for the crown. They had both assumed that young Lance would happily leap into the adventure with them.

They were wrong.

Lance watched the search for the mythic doo dad kill his friend's father. The professor had died of a heart attack, but it was his defeat over not finding his prize that ultimately did him in. Lance feared that the same fate awaited his father and his friend and he decided to have no part of it.

It caused a rift between Lance and Simon that took many years to heal. It was another mutual friend, Red Davis, who helped the boys bury the hatchet.

The division between father and son was less deep, but they eventually got past it and the Star boys had many adventures of their own seeking the lost treasures of the world. It was on one of those trips where Landon, Lance, Simon, and Red met Buck Tellonger. They had come to Bangladesh following a lead on a major artifact. Though they all almost died at least once on this caper, they returned home with a valuable treasure and a new friend in Buck Tellonger. They became fast friends and shared several other adventures over the years.

Then war broke out and the world fell into chaos.

With what would later come to be called World War I heating up, Buck returned to military service for his country while Landon and his son, now a teenager, returned home to the United States. It would be a few years before Buck would meet up with Lance again, but sadly he never saw his friend, Landon again.

Once again on the trail of the Crown of Gengis Kai, the latest information he had collected pointed toward Cairo. Landon loaded the plane and flew off in search of his greatest find alone.

He did not return.

Learning of his friend's disappearance, Buck Telonger returned to the United States where he became Lance's guardian, as stipulated in Landon's will. He never tried to replace his father, but Buck Tellonger was the closest thing to a parent Lance had in this world. Once he was of legal age, Lance started Lance Star, Inc. and started construction of Star Field. Buck accepted a generous offer from him to join the family business as Vice President and second in command of the Sky Rangers.

And now, once again, the Crown of Gengis Kai had put Lance and his friends in danger.

Lance pulled his friend over to a less traveled section of the lobby and they each took a seat. Lance then pulled a large potted plant that sported a plant with big leaves closer to block them from full view.

"Why are we waiting?" Simon asked, breaking Lance's trip down memory lane.

"We are probably the two most wanted people in this country right now," Lance said softly. "You do understand that, right? If they aren't here already, and if they aren't, then I've really underestimated The Overlord, then they will be here shortly."

"How would they know to look here?"

"Did you sign in under your own name? Did you pay in cash and use an alias or did you put it under the university's name?"

"Well, I…"

"Doesn't matter," Lance said. "Your hotel room isn't going to be hard to find."

"I don't understand," Simon started to protest.

A lifelong student, Simon had never had to live in the real world as it existed outside of his safe, university-controlled bubble. The only time he was off campus was when he went on a dig, but even there he was surrounded by university personnel and security. He had no real understanding of how things worked.

"We'll take the stairs. Come on."

"But we need the key," Simon said.

"We'll manage," Lance said and ushered his friend into the stairwell.

The fourteenth floor was empty.

Lance eased open the stairwell door and looked for any sign of guards or agents on the prowl. So far, they had managed to remain a few steps ahead of the agents after them. It was only the narrowest of leads and Lance did not want to hang around any longer than necessary.

"Let's go," he whispered.

They walked to Simon's room.

"Fourteen Oh One," Simon said as he pointed to the closed door. "If we only had a key."

Lance tried the door handle.

It was locked.

He pulled a small leather pouch from his back pocket and removed two small black pieces of metal.

"What are those?" Simon asked.

Lance smiled. "They're for unlocking locked doors without a key. A friend of mine taught me how to use these a while back. I've been looking forward to trying it out in the wild."

"Interesting," Simon said, leaning in close to watch.

"You're in my light," Lance said.

"Sorry."

It only took a minute or two, but eventually there was a soft click and the door unlocked. Smiling, Lance turned the knob and pushed the door open slowly.

"Impressive," Simon said.

"You'd be amazed how often I find myself needing to get inside a locked room," Lance joked as they went inside. "Now, where are your notes?"

"In the closet. Over there." He pointed.

"Okay. Good. Grab them and let's get moving."

"You really think they're going to come after us here?"

"Oh, I'm quite sure of it," Lance said as soon as he saw the room's primary entrance open again. Unlike Lance and Simon, the new arrival had a key.

The man charged into the room the moment he saw Lance standing there. From his trench coat covered suit and tie and the sunglasses and hat he wore, the man was obviously an agent of The Overlord. The three men they had squared off against inside the Great and Powerful club wore similar outfits.

This man was bulkier than the other three Lance and company had encountered.

He was a fighter.

Lance barely had time to move before the big man slammed into him. He pivoted, trying his best to dodge and attack simultaneously. It was a move he had employed before. Sometimes it worked.

Then there were times like this one.

The agent hit lance with all the severity of a bull plowing into a matador. The impact pushed Lance off balance and he and the agent fell over the bed in the center of the room, crashing to the floor on the far side, tangled together in a mess of arms and legs. Both men kept fighting, punching and kicking at their opponent.

Lance was able to land a punch to the big man's nose, snapping the thick plastic frames of his dark glasses and breaking the man's nose.

The agent tried to stand with the bed serving to steady him.

Lance had no plans to offer him time to recover.

Still on the floor, Lance brought his knees close to his chest then kicked out hard, pushing the agent backward over the corner of the bed, blood splattering across the wall.

Lance was on his feet in a shot.

Before the injured agent could recover, the pilot grabbed a fistful of the man's coat and lifted him bodily from the floor.

The agent spat blood.

Lance punched him in the face.

Now unconscious, Lance lowered the agent back to the floor.

"Are you okay?" Simon said from near the closet door. He held a satchel filled with his notes.

"I'll live," Lance said. "Time to move, Simon! There are most likely more on the way!"

Simon started toward the door that led to the hallway.

"Not that way," his friend shouted.

Lance pointed toward the double doors that lead out onto the balcony overlooking the city and the mountains beyond.

"This way."

After throwing open the doors, the American adventurer stepped out cautiously. He wanted to make certain there were no snipers lying in wait to take either of them out. So far, as best he could tell, they wanted Simon alive. Lance wasn't sure what his status was with The Overlord.

He had run afoul of men like the one who ruled this tiny island nation before. They were also slick talkers, bullies with a little money and influence to keep them in power. To defeat men like The Overlord, all you had to do was remove their influence and they could be taken down easily enough. Bullies were only effective until the one being bullied fought back.

Lance and the Sky Rangers were known for standing against bullies. They usually did so on a global stage, but Lance Star was no fan of bullies wherever they resided.

"How do you plan to get us out of here?" Simon asked.

"Remember that time you, me, and Red got into a scrape in Cairo?"

"Ah, yes," Simon said. "Jasmine."

"Right. Jasmine."

Lance chuckled at the memory.

"Remember how we got out of her room in the palace?"

"I'm too old to jump off a balcony," Simon said. "And we're fourteen stories up. Jasmine's room was on the fourth floor. There's a big difference there!"

"Yeah. A bit. Trust me, okay?"

"Why stop now," Simon said.

Lance pointed to the balcony for the neighboring room.

"It's an easy step over. Then we go to the next. From there, it's an easy drop to the next building over."

"For a pilot, you know a lot about getting out of tight spots on the ground," Simon joked as he climbed over to the next balcony.

"You'd be amazed how often this sort of thing happens," Lance quipped as he followed.

###

"Did you see which way they went?"

"I'm sorry, sir. I did not."

When Agent Sunday had arrived at the hotel room rented to archaeologist Simon Prentiss, he had expected to find the good professor and take him into custody. Barring that, the hope had been to collect the man's research and return it to The Overlord as ordered.

Walking in to find one of his agents unconscious did not leave the best impression.

"What happened, Agent Monday?" he asked, his exasperation with the man's performance shining through.

"When I came to check out the room, as instructed, I found a man in the room already."

"Simon Prentiss?"

"No," the agent said, pinching his nose to stop the blood flow. "It was the other man. The one who fled the club with the professor."

"Lance Star?"

"I believe that is his name, yes, sir."

"And he did this to you?"

"He got lucky, sir," Monday said. "Caught me off guard, but I gave as good as I got."

"No doubt," Sunday said with disdain. "Not enough to stop him, but perhaps enough to slow him down."

"Maybe."

"Maybes are for the uninitiated, Agent Monday. As a member of The Overlord's police force, you should always know. Maybe is not acceptable. You should know this by now."

"I apologize," Monday said.

"You still have a chance to redeem yourself," Sunday said.

"Sir?"

"I have been recalled to The Overlord's office. I am leaving a small detachment of soldiers here, under your command. Your only concern right now is to find Simon Prentiss and bring him to The Overlord."

"And if Lance Star intervenes again?"

"Kill him."

9.

Buck Tellonger hurt all over.

Between the bar fight, crouching in the bushes outside the airfield, and getting popped in the face with a slapper, he had taken a good bot of punishment and he was starting to feel all of it. He remained still, hoping that the pain would ease if he didn't move. He even kept his eyes shut. The last thing he wanted was to tip off the men who had taken him that he was no longer out cold.

"Wake him," he heard an unfamiliar voice say.

So much for that plan, Buck thought.

There was a small *pop* followed by the familiar sharp ammonia sting of smelling salts. It was impossible to fake being out once the ammonia vapors hit the sinuses.

Buck coughed and sat up.

He shook the cobwebs from his brain and took in his surroundings.

The room was an office. Not the small, cluttered eight by ten-foot box he called an office back at Star Field that was only big enough to hold a desk, two chairs, a filing cabinet, and a coat rack. No, this was the office of a head of state, which made sense when he realized who the man standing at the far end of the office was, even before he spoke.

"Welcome back to the land of the living, Mr. Tellonger.," the man wearing the expensive tailor-made suit and jacket said without turning. Instead, he continued staring out the window at the city below.

His city.

"If it's all the same to you, I could have used another couple hours of shut eye," Buck said as he struggled to stand. His legs were still asleep and refused to cooperate.

Two of the agents lifted him up and pushed him into a chair across from a large, antique desk. They were less than gentle.

"Easy," Buck said, defaulting to obstinate as he shot the agent nearest him his dirtiest look.

"Settle down," the agent grunted.

Before Buck could stand back up, the agents pushed him back into the cushioned chair. He struggled against them, but they had the advantage in numbers and leverage.

"Mr. Tellonger, please. There is no use in attempting to flee," the well-dressed man said as he turned to face his prisoner. "There's nowhere to run to, I assure you."

"Who's running?" Buck sniped back. "I was planning to teach your boys here some manners. That's all."

"I'm sure," the man said. "I take it you know who I am?"

"You're the big man around these parts. Like to call yourself The Overlord. A bit pompous, if you ask me, but an accurate moniker, I suppose."

"You're fairly glib for a man this close to oblivion," The Overlord said. "Surely, you realize the depths of the danger you're in."

"What I know is that your goons picked a fight earlier. Then, later, they hit me upside the noggin. That tells me they aren't good enough to take me in a fair fight."

"What's a fair fight?"

"You got me there," Buck said around a sly smile. "I can play just as dirty as the next guy."

"I'm sure you can."

"Hey! I just realized something," Buck exclaimed. "You're not from around these parts, are you? You're not Magnapor-born. You're an American."

"Can't sneak anything past you, can I, Mr. Tellonger?" The Overlord said around a chuckle.

The Overlord was tall and handsome, with chiseled features. His dark hair was just starting to streak through with a stray gray hair or three, just enough to make him look distinguished. Buck understood. He had been seeing more and more of those stray white hairs in his own mustache of late and did not like it one bit. The Overlord didn't seem to mind, but he clearly had a few years on the pilot. Perhaps he had simply gotten used to them.

"You are correct. I am an American. John Mason, at your service."

He held out a hand, but Buck made no move to reach out to shake it. He wasn't convinced the agents would have let him even if he tried.

"I was born in Montana and eventually migrated to New York," Mason said. "That's where I attended college and started my first business. Within five years I made my first million. The world, as they say, was my oyster."

"I'm guessing that oyster must have been hot if you had to hightail it out of the states."

The Overlord grimaced, which only spurred Buck's taunts.

"Let me guess… Drugs? Weapons? Were you running girls or maybe booze during prohibition? Come on, Mason. I'm honestly curious. What kind of criminal are you?"

"Land, Mr. Tellonger. I was in real estate. Acquiring land is my skill."

"Buying and selling land isn't illegal?" Buck reminded him.

"It depends on who you buy the land for and then how it is then used."

"And the best you could do was buy a volcano and plant a city on it?" Buck said. "That's not really all that smart, is it? I mean, it sounds like something a villain out of an old pulp novel might try. Is that the kind of villain you are, Mr. Overlord?"

The Overlord smiled.

"Magnapor is my little slice of paradise. Of all the properties I own, this place is where I think of when I think of home. Volcano aside, Magnapor is paradise."

"Unless you're one of the poor people who was here first."

The Overlord's smile faded. "I am not to blame for their lot in life. If you cannot become successful on your own, then you deserve whatever fate befalls you."

"Uh, huh," Buck said. "When you announced yourself Overlord of this island, those people became your responsibility. You tax them, don't you?"

"Of course. No one lives on my island for free."

"Then you're the government here. Last time I checked it was the government's job to help its citizenry."

"Are you really so naive, Mr. Tellonger? When I decided I wanted this island, I paid off the government that was already in place. They were a cruel regime. Citizens were rounded up in the night and shot at dawn. There were people dying in the streets. Starvation was epidemic."

"You helped them, is that it?"

"Yes."

"In exchange for what?"

"Loyalty," The Overlord said. "I bought this island furnished, as we like to say back in the real estate game. That means I bought the dirt, the rocks, the buildings, the volcano, and yes, even the people. They all belong to me."

"They must be so thrilled."

"I eliminated the firing squads. I shut down the debtor's prison and made sure everyone had a way to earn their keep. Many own their own businesses. I assume you've seen our excellent bazaar?"

"As flea markets go, it ain't bad," Buck snorted.

"Those who do not share the entrepreneurial spirit of their fellows are given other options. They can go to work either in the fields that grow our food or take civil service positions working in government offices, sweeping the streets, collecting garbage..."

"Gestapo agents?" Buck said, chucking a thumb over his shoulder to the two government agents behind him.

"You're a funny man, Mr. Tellonger."

"Laughing's easy when you've got stupid people to make fun of, herr Overlord."

"Droll," The Overlord said.

Buck shrugged.

"I figured a man with your background... that's right, I did my research on you, Mr. Tellonger. Before the war turned you into a hero of the Allies, you were a bad boy. Smuggler, thief, muscle. If you had been more successful at any of those jobs, who knows, you might own your own island."

The Overlord shrugged.

"But the war did happen and I changed," Buck said matter-of-fact. "In fact, I fought a war against men just like you, Mr. Mason. The uniform is different, pin stripes instead of jodhpurs, but that doesn't make you any less a bad guy, now does it?"

"You're correct, Mr. Tellonger," The Overlord said as he lit a cigarette. "I am, as you say, a bad guy. You would do well to remember that fact."

"I'm not afraid of you," Buck said plainly. "Do your worst. You can only kill me once."

"On any other day, I might take you up on that challenge," The Overlord said. "However, you caught me on a good day. I will let you and your friend, the hero pilot, Lance Star leave this island alive and healthy. Perhaps with even a bit more coin in your pocket than when you arrived."

"You think you can buy Lance Star?" Buck said, nearly choking on the words. "Boy, if you think that'll work, you're in for a big surprise. I've never met a more honest person that Lance. He's the ultimate Boy Scout."

"Lucky for me, I have a Plan B."

"And that would be?"

"Do you really expect me to tell you my plans, Mr. Tellonger?"

"I think you like to hear yourself talk, Mason. See, I think you've bought into this fantasy you've concocted around yourself." He raised his voice as if announcing a new movie serial. "The Overlord! Dread pirate kind of the Seven Seas! Ruler of deadly Magnapor!"

"It has a nice ring to it, don't you think?"

"I think you like to see yourself as the villain, a dangerous man who holds the lives of every man, woman, and child on this island in the palm of his hands. It makes you feel powerful... untouchable."

"Have you seen anything to dispute that description?"

"No," Buck said, not bothering to hide his disdain. "It sounds like you're looking for some hero to beat. You want to show all comers that you are the biggest, baddest man in these waters. What better way to do that than to go up against a world-wide celebrity like Lance Star? If you take him down, your reputation would be solidified."

Buck leaned back in his chair and waited.

"Who's aiming their sites at you?" Buck asked. "Have you made an enemy out o someone who isn't afraid of you?"

"Look round, Mr. Tellonger. The entire world stands on the brink of another blasted war. The last one nearly destroyed us. You were there. You saw first-hand what this kind of chaos creates. I fear that the fuse has already been lit. War is on the horizon and when massive nation-states go to war, small islands like mine are gobbled up in the carnage and men like me…"

The Overlord turned and looked back out the window.

"Men like me are lined up against a wall and shot."

"Heavy is the head that wears the crown," Buck joked.

The Overlord spun back and gave him a dirty look.

"So that's it. You're after the professor's little crown, aren't you? Please don't tell me you believe tat nonsense."

"The Crown of Gengis Kai may or may not be magical in origin, but that doesn't matter. The power of the crown is in its legend. The crown holds sway over those who believe, Mr. Tellonger, and you are standing on an island full of superstitious believers. If I hold the crown, not only do I solidify my role as leader of the people of Magnapor, but outsiders will think twice about tempting fate."

"You're an idiot."

The Overlord moved quickly.

Buck barely had time to brace himself before the businessman's punch caught him on the cheek. He spit out a small amount of blood. He'd bitten his cheek.

"Thanks for proving my point," Buck said around a pained wince. "You've been keeping tabs on the professor so he can lead you to the treasure."

"That was the plan. Yes."

"Then why bring us here?"

"Sadly, that was not part of my plan. My agents were directed to intercept any communications off the island. I did not want him talking to anyone outside of the island. My agents failed to follow my instructions. They have been dealt with... harshly."

"Good help is so hard to find these days."

"That's where you come in," The Overlord said.

"What? You might want to lay off smoking whatever the local blend is around these parts, pal." Buck said. "You know I'm not going to help you track down my friend. You can threaten, bribe, and even cajole, but I can guarantee you this much, you will get absolutely no help from me, Mason."

"Good thing for me that your help is not why I had you brought here."

"It's not?" Buck asked, puzzled. "Then what the hell do you want from me?"

"You are leverage, Mr. Tellonger. You see, I already know where your friends are going. In fact, you and I will be joining them shortly."

"Then what...?"

"From your reputations, I can safely surmise that neither you or Lance Star would willing surrender the crown. I also suspect that you would both lay down your life for the other. Am I correct?"

"You've not said anything to dispute that description," Buck said, parroting back the man's own words.

"And that is why you are here. Your partner will not stand idly by and allow you to die. Once he and Professor Prentiss find the Crown of Gengis Kai, Lance Star is going to trade it to me in exchange for you, Mr. Tellonger."

"I wouldn't bet even money on that."

"You underestimate yourself, Mr. Tellonger. The two of you are in the newsreels so often that it's hard not to get the sense of who you are. Lance Star will give me what I want or you, he, and Simon Prentiss will never leave this island alive."

###

Lance Star knew something was wrong.

The hangar was empty. It was also being watched.

Lance had spotted one of The Overlord's secret police nearby. He was concealed well enough that Lance might not have noticed him. Then he lit a cigarette and revealed his position to anyone on or near the airfield hangars.

Lance told Simon to head for the hangar while he took care of the agent. Simon Prentiss was many things, but stealthy was not one of his many talents.

As bait, however, that was a role he was perfectly capable of handling.

As soon as he reached the door and went inside, the agent moved in to follow him. He tossed his cigarette onto the pavement and reached for the door.

That's when Lance made his move.

The agent did not see him coming and the fight was ended before it even begun.

Lance pulled the unconscious agent into the hangar by his arms, the heel of his shoes scuffing the concrete as they were pulled along. Once he was locked in the tiny utility closet, Lance ushered his childhood friend on board the cargo plane.

"This isn't what I expected," Simon said as he strapped into the co-pilot's chair.

Lance climbed into the pilot's chair to his left and started pre-light warm-up. "What exactly were you expecting?"

"This seems a little common for you is all. I've seen the newsreel footage. You build some pretty birds in that manufacturing plant of yours."

"You wanted to see the Skybolt II, didn't you?"

"I really did."

"You're the one who asked for us to come in stealthy and whatnot so, if you want to take a ride in the Skybolt, you're going to have to come by Star Field in New York. I'll give you the best view of the city, guaranteed."

"Once the crown is safely locked away, you've got yourself a deal."

"Are we not going to wait for your friend, Mr. Tellonger? I thought he was supposed to meet us here?"

"He was," Lance said, trying not to worry. "That guy was watching our hangar. It's a good bet Buck might have had another run in with them. If he's not here, there's a good reason for it."

"You think he's in trouble?"

"Maybe. Look, Buck is a bulldog. It takes a lot for him to be in trouble. Let's go find your treasure and then we'll go looking for Buck. With any luck, he'll meet us on the way."

"If you're sure."

"Too late to do anything about it now."

Lance Star pushed the throttle and the cargo plane rolled slowly out of the hangar into the open sky. A quick turn put him on the airstrip's hardtop. Another quick push and the plane accelerated faster and faster toward the end of the runway.

"We've got company!" Simon shouted as two cars bearing the official seal of the Magnapor police pulled into the airfield.

"Too late now," Lance called out as the plane lifted off the ground and soared toward the heavens. They were home free.

For the moment.

"Okay, Simon. It's your show. I need coordinates or a direction."

Simon Prentiss flipped through the pages of his notebook, nodding and humming as he scanned the pages.

"North. Our landing coordinates are on the other side of the volcano."

"Of course, it is," Lance mumbled.

Once again, Lance Star felt a queasy sensation tighten in his gut.

"For a second there, I almost forgot about the volcano," he said as he flew straight toward it.

10.

"Where are we going, Simon?"

Professor Simon Prentiss flipped through his notes. "According to my research, the crown was placed in a chamber inside a fortress that was enveloped by lava during the last great eruption over a few hundred years ago."

"So, you're saying it's inside a cooled lava flow?" Lance Star asked, trying to keep his frustration from spilling out. "Over half of this island is a lava flow, Simon! You got any way of narrowing that down some?"

"Would coordinates help?"

"Yes," Lance said, hopeful.

"Well, I don't have coordinates," Simon said.

The pilot sighed.

"Oh, come on, Lance. You know how this works," Simon said. "Neither archaeology nor treasure hunting is that easy. There's never an easily comprehensible map leading right to it. X never marks the spot."

"Don't remind me," Lance said. "I remember following you and dad all over hell's north forty in search of one trinket or another. A map definitely would have been helpful."

"But how can there be a map to something that's lost?" Simon said, smiling. "Besides, that would make it too easy."

"Well, we can't have that."

"Where would be the fun in that?"

"You and I have very different ideas about what constitutes '*fun*,' my friend."

"Noted."

"Can you at least narrow it down?"

"Now that I can do," Simon said, unfurling a map in his lap. "The war between Gengis Kai and the Warriors of Hades was fought on the north end of the island. Eyewitness testimony from Gengis Kai's men on their sailing ships reports that they were battling atop the mouth of the volcano when it erupted."

"On top of…"

"Don't start. You know how legends are, Lance. They're full of metaphors and romanticized versions of the truth to make the story more appealing."

"Let's not forget that they get more outlandish with each telling," the pilot reminded his friend. "You know that urban legends are almost as often fiction as they are facts, even if it's romanticized fiction."

"I know, but they all have their roots in reality," Prentiss countered. "We know for a fact that the volcano did erupt here around the same time that Gengis Kai was reportedly active here. We know that a battle of some kind was fought here."

"Against lava monsters?"

"Maybe not," Prentiss relented. "That could have been a combination of factors from armor type to a trick of the light."

"Makes sense."

"Or it could be exactly what it sounds like. Tell me, Lance, honestly, in all your many adventures, have you never run across something that couldn't be easily explained away?"

Lance shook his head. "I can't say that. We've seen some out there things. Some of them I still can't wrap my head around. There are unexplained events."

"Then why can't the Warriors of Hades also be true?"

"I wish I had an answer for you, pal," Lance said.

####

It wasn't the smoothest landing he had ever made, but Lance Star put the plane down with minimal issues. The ground was uneven in places. Not uncommon considering that most of the surface was made of cooled molten lava with a dusting of topsoil on top that allowed grass and weeds to grow. Even under such harsh conditions, life found a way to thrive.

Lance and Simon Prentiss grabbed their gear and exited the plane.

"The view is breathtaking," Simon said.

The old friends looked out over the Pacific Ocean below as white frothy waves crashed against dense rock formations that had once been molten lava before it cooled. In their travels, these two, along with Lance's late father, found themselves in some of the world's most interesting locales. Sometimes, like now, they were surrounded by beauty, but usually, there was danger lurking around every corner, evil hiding in every shadow.

Sadly, Magnapor was more the latter. Danger was all around them. Lance could feel it closing in on them, but the view was beautiful. There was no denying that.

"The intense cold of the ocean and the heat of the lava flash-solidified the lava into rock," Simon explained. "With each new eruption, the island's perimeter grows a few meters."

"Fascinating," Lance said. "Not my first active volcano, Simon. Remember?"

"Right. Sorry."

"Do we have any idea when this one is expected to blow?" Lance asked.

"No idea," Simon said. "This region is unstable so it could be any time… or it could be never."

"Well, me being here certainly ratchets up the odds against us," Lance said, only half joking. "I've never stepped foot near an active volcano that didn't erupt while we were there."

"Seriously?"

Lance shrugged. "I swear, you'd think my life is a pulp novel some of the crap we run into."

"I follow your exploits. Your life is a pulp novel, pal," Simon snorted.

"All the more reason to pick up the pace. Let's get this crown of yours, find Buck, and get the hell off this island."

"I'm for that."

"Lead on, Professor," Lance said, motioning for his friend to take the lead.

With a nod, Simon Prentiss moved ahead, checking his compass, folded map, and his hand-written journal notes to lead him toward the cavern entrance.

"That way," he pointed.

"On your six," Lance said and fell into step behind him.

The search lasted the better part of an hour. Professor Prentiss' notes were extensive, but they were also based on the island of Magnapor as it existed a few hundred years earlier. Ever the romantic, Simon Prentiss incorporated legend and folklore into his studies along with historical facts. He wanted to believe that the fantastical was as real as the rest. Lance was more the pragmatist, an odd position to take considering all of the things he had witnessed firsthand in his travels.

Lance remembered dogfighting with a Nazi-controlled pterodactyl, for heaven's sake. He knew the fantastical existed. Why was he finding it so hard to believe what his father and friend believed in regards to Gengis Kai and his super-powered crown?

Compared to things he's witnessed, was the story of the crown really that far-fetched?

Lance couldn't argue the point so decided to stop arguing with Simon and back his friend's play. If they found the crown, Lance would be the first to eat crow.

"There it is!" Simon shouted.

Lance followed his friend's wild gestures toward a large outcropping that bulged over the edge of the island. As they made their way closer, Lance could see the opening of a cave hidden by the off shape of the lava flow. From a distance, you couldn't tell it was a cave.

"My, my, my," Lance said. "Hidden in plain sight."

"The best treasures usually are," Simon said with pride. "Come on."

"Now, hold on there, Pecos Bill. Let's not rush in blindly."

"You're right," Simon said, though he showed no signs of slowing down.

Igniting his lantern, Professor Prentiss entered the cave.

Lance turned on his flashlight and followed.

The cavern was remarkable easy to navigate, a detail that gave Lance pause. Like his friend, the pilot had also visited his fair share of caves, caverns, and hidden tunnels. He had even been inside the lava tubes of a volcano once, just minutes ahead of an eruption. All of them were far more harrowing than this cave.

"You're imagining things, Lance," Simon said when his friend mentioned his misgivings. "Sometimes we get lucky."

"Really?"

"Well, usually not this lucky, I admit, but I try not to look good fortune in the mouth."

"Then let's be cautious, if nothing…" Lance started as the cave in front of them opened into a larger chamber.

"…else," the ace pilot said, his voice trailing off.

At the far edge of the chamber sat a throne carved out of molten rock and polished until it glistened like black glass. Their lights reflected off the shiny surface.

Sitting on the throne was the mummified remains of a man, a very tall man. Dried skin clung to old bones under tattered cloth remains. Whoever the man was, he had died elsewhere and was posed in the seated position on the black throne.

In his lap sat a box, a chest carved out of pure silver and adorned with gold and jewels, each of which were as polished as the throne. Dust filled every corner of the room except the throne.

"You believe me now?"

"I have to admit, I had my doubts."

Simon held his lantern high and the light reflected off the gold crown that sat atop the mummified warrior's head.

"Is that…" Lance asked.

"Right where they said he would be," Prentiss said.

"Where who said?"

Simon Prentiss ignored his companion and stepped closer to the throne.

"Right where who said, Simon?"

"Gengis Kai's men," Simon said. He tapped the pages in his notebook. "A couple of years ago, I found the remains of a wrecked ship that was rumored to be part of Gengis Kai's fleet. In the captain's quarters was a journal that described the burial site of Gengis Kai. What was missing was the logbook that showed where they had been. I always assumed Magnapor was the beginning of the search to recover the crown. I never expected to find it here."

Simon reached out to touch the crown.

"And so well preserved."

"Wait," Lance shouted, blocking the professor from his find.

"What is wrong with you, Lance?"

"Does this not seem too easy to you?" the pilot said.

"Well…"

"Look at how clean this is, Simon. Either someone else knows about this place and visits often or it's booby trapped."

"You've seen too many movie serials," Simon said.

"And you've read a lot of books, Simon. You know as well as I do that traps to keep out graverobbers are far more common than most people think."

"But it's right there! All I have to do is…"

Simon pulled the crown from the mummified head.

"…this!"

Nothing happened.

Simon let out a laugh, relieved.

"I can't believe you did that," Lance said, trying to slow his rapid heartbeat.

"I can't believe it worked," Simon said, smiling as he stared at his prize.

"You know, I really can't believe it either," a deep timbered voice called out from behind them.

Lance and Simon spun at the sound of the new arrival's voice.

They were met with another sound, this one far more familiar, the sound of weapons chambering rounds.

Standing at the entrance to the chamber was a tall man in an expensive suit. Surrounded as he was by men in trench coats matching the ones worn by The Overlord's secret police, Lance could easily guess his identity.

"The Overlord, I presume?"

"Right the first time, Mr. Star."

"You know my name. I'm flattered."

The Overlord smiled. "Your friend, Mr. Tellonger, has told me all about you. I feel as though I already know you and Professor Prentiss so well."

"What have you done with Buck?" Lance said, taking a step forward.

"I assure you, he's quite unharmed," The Overlord said, snapping his fingers.

Seconds later, Buck was escorted in under guard, his hands bound behind his back.

"You okay?" Lance asked.

"I'll live."

"Touching," The Overlord said. "Now that the niceties are concluded, I have come to collect my prize."

"Your what?" Lance asked.

"Professor Prentiss, bring me the Crown of Gengis Kai."

11.

"I will take my prize now," The Overlord said.

"It doesn't belong to you," Lance Star said, stepping between The Overlord and Simon Prentiss. "Now, you let my friend go and maybe we can talk this out."

"I don't think so, Mr. Star."

"Posturing won't help you," Lance said. "I've gone up against much bigger bad guys than you. You may call yourself The Overlord, but at the end of the day, you're just another egomaniacal jerk in a tailored suit."

The Overlord chuckled.

"I don't think you grasp the full picture," The Overlord said, taking a couple of leisurely steps forward. "It's not the fact that my men have you surrounded, which they do. It's not even the point that I have your friend in custody, but I do."

He motioned toward Buck.

The agent of Magnapor's secret police guarding Lance's friend kicked the pilot behind the knee, sending Buck Tellonger crashing to the floor, hands tied behind his back and a gun pointed at his head.

"The concept you seem to have trouble grasping, Mr. Star is that this…"

His gestured to take in everything around them.

"All of this, this entire island, belongs to me. Lock, stock, and barrel, Magnapor Island is mine. Not only do I own the earth beneath your feet, but everything on this island belongs to me as well. This cave is my property. These men are my property. The Crown of Gengis Kai is mine as well."

The Overlord smiled.

"In fact, you, Mr. American hero, became my property the moment you illegally set foot on my island."

"That'll be the day, pal!"

Clucking his teeth, The Overlord waggled a finger in front of his opponent.

"No. No. This is not the time for your macho American theatrics. Oh, yes. I know all about you, Mr. Star. I have seen you and Mr. Tellonger there in the newsreels. You two, along with your squadron of, what do you call them? Ah, yes, Sky Rangers, no? I see you wave to the cheering crowds and accepting the accolades of your government for flying all around the world and imposing your imperialist American agenda on tiny, innocent nations such as mine."

"Are you insane?" Simon Prentiss shouted.

"Easy, Simon," Lance warned.

"And now, you have come here to steal from me," The Overlord continued, pulling a gun from his shoulder holster and pointing it at Lance and Simon. "I'm afraid I cannot let that stand."

"Simon's right. You are crazy!"

"No. Not crazy. Poor people are crazy, Mr. Star. I am the leader of my people and absolute ruler of this island. I decide what is or is not considered crazy on this island."

"Okay, so insane it is then," Buck said.

The agent kicked him in the side and Buck fell over onto his stomach, face in the dirt. He groaned under the impact.

The agent kicked him once more for good measure.

"Stop it!" Lance shouted, taking a step forward.

Another agent stepped forward and pointed a cocked gun at the pilot's forehead.

"I wouldn't do that, if I were you, Mr. Star," The Overlord said as if admonishing a child.

Lance stopped, both eyes focused on the gun pointed at him.

"Professor Prentiss, I will have the crown now," The Overlord commanded.

"No!"

"Step back, gentlemen," The Overlord said, motioning them away from the polished thrown and the mummified remains of the man history knew as Gengis Kai.

"You don't understand," Prentiss started, but The Overlord silenced him quickly.

"Not another word, Professor. I will not warn you again."

"You heard the man, Simon," Lance said, easing his fried away from the throne.

"But, Lance…"

"Just do it," Lance muttered. "Don't argue."

The Overlord stood before the throne where Gengis Kai and his crown had been placed at the time of his death. He returned the gun to his holster and then examined the remains, running a hand over the dark, polished stone.

"Simply remarkable," he said. "To think, this powerful relic has been right here, hidden in plain sight all this time."

The Overlord reached for the crown.

"No!" Simon Prentiss shouted. He took a step forward, but Lance held him back.

"I warned you, professor…"

The Overlord's fingers wrapped around the crown and he lifted it gently off of its owner's petrified scalp.

"At least," The Overlord said, a wide smile cleaving his face. "The power! It's mine!"

"You fool!"

"Not the time, Simon," Lance warned.

"You don't understand!"

"Oh, I understand all too well, professor," The Overlord said.

Entranced, he held the crown in front of him as he admired its simplistic beauty. In all of the historical documents Simon Prentiss had studied, in all of the stories he had listened to spoken aloud, the look of the crown was constantly evolving. Some described it as an ornately decorated crown made of solid gold while others purported it to be platinum or any other rare metal.

The truth, by comparison was a letdown.

The crown was gold, though a thin sheet of gold, unpolished, and scuffed by years of abuse and the ravages of time. Large palm fronds from some local plant were woven into the crown, giving it the appearance of a tiki statue. There were no jewels decorating the crown.

In modern terms, it was worth whatever small amount of gold could be melted from it, which wasn't much. The crown's real power came from the legend that surrounded it. Neither Lance nor Simon suspected there was true supernatural power in the crown. The greatest value it held was from a historical perspective. It was proof that a man calling himself Gengis Kai truly existed.

"The crown isn't magic," Lance said, trying to get through to The Overlord.

His words fell on deaf ears.

Before he could try again, a tremor ran through the ground beneath the pilot's feet.

Lance looked down and saw small pebbles dancing across the cavern floor.

"Oh, crap," he muttered.

"What is…" The Overlord started.

"It's boobytrapped, you moron!" Simon shouted.

Cracks splintered through the hard stone, sending gouts of steam into the cavern and throwing tiny slivers of rock in all directions.

A large explosion happened far below, sending everyone to the ground.

The Overlord lost his grip on the crown and it slid across the cavern floor, bouncing along its uneven surface.

Buck Tellonger took advantage of the chaos. He swiped a leg out and knocked the legs out from under the agent who was guarding him.

The man hit the deck hard.

Buck was on him in a shot with a knee on the man's neck until he passed out. As soon as the man stopped struggling, Buck pulled the knife off the agent's belt and cut his bonds.

His hands free, Buck looked for his friends.

Lance was pushing Simon to safety, not that Buck saw too many safe spots in the cave. Cracks continues to break open across the floor and ceiling. Some pieces of rock fell from the ceiling and shattered when they hit the bottom.

"Time to go, boss!" Buck shouted as he ran over to join them.

"No one leaves!" The Overlord shouted. The crown was once more clenched in his white-knuckled grasp.

"You don't understand," Simon said.

Before The Overlord could respond, the rumble beneath their feet intensified, sending everyone to the ground, no longer able to stand on the violently shifting ground.

Somehow, The Overlord kept his grip on the crown.

"Boss! Look!" Buck Tellonger shouted.

Lance Star followed his friend's gaze and his heart fell into his stomach.

"We've got a new problem," he whispered.

"What are you…" Prentiss started, but then he saw what worried his friend so and his eyes grew wide in shock and terror.

Molten lava poured from the cracks in the stone walls as if the tomb of Gengis Kai was bleeding. The temperature rose exponentially as the fiery liquid began pooling around the risers in the uneven cave floor.

"Oh, how I hate it when I'm right," Lance muttered. "Time to go, Simon," he said, grabbing his friend by the arm.

"But the crown…"

"Lost cause, pal! In a choice between us and the crown, I choose us each time! We have got to go!"

Simon wanted to pull away, to argue, but he knew Lance was right. Their fathers had both lost their lives in search of the Crown of Gengis Kai. Neither of them had been able to prove its existence, much less bring it home. At least Simon Prentiss could say that he had seen it with his own eyes.

"Damn! I wish I had a camera!"

"So, do I," Buck said, pointing toward the lava bleeding from the walls.

The flow had slowed.

"What could cause that?"

"Oh, Simon. I wish you hadn't asked that," Lance said.

"Why?"

Lance pointed as the cracks widened, the sharp pop and crack of shattering stone echoing off the cavern walls around them.

"That's why!" Lance shouted.

"Holy…" Buck said, his voice fading in the din of crushing rock.

"Is that?" Simon asked, unable to completely comprehend what he was seeing.

"My God…" Lance muttered.

Lance Star had dismissed the legends out of hand. He had seen many things that defied explanation in his short career, but never had he seen anything like the strange scenario playing out in front of him. It wasn't the lava. This wasn't his first time standing on a volcano as it decided to erupt. In fact, this was his third active eruption.

It wasn't the collapsing ceiling or enemy agents with guns. No. Lance and his crew had faced these type of threats before and thrived.

What he saw in front of him now, challenged the air ace's beliefs to their core and he felt shame. He felt deep shame for not believing his father or his friend when they first told him the legend of Gengis Kai. The story was preposterous and grew only more so with each retelling. Lance could not believe that sentient beings made out of molten lava were real. That defied all of the laws of nature he understood.

Walking, talking rock men was a flight of fancy too far.

But yet, as he watched those very same creatures he had denied could truly exist step out of the cracks in the wall with molten hot lava rolling off of their rock-encrusted forms like water rolled off the back of a duck, Lance Star could no longer deny the truth.

The Warriors of Hades were not just creatures of legend.

They were real.

And they were standing right in front of Lance Star and his friends.

12.

Lance Star couldn't believe his eyes.

Over the years, he had witnessed some truly remarkable events. Some of them were even hard to rationalize to himself, much less explain to others. His definition of *normal* changed on a regular basis these days. Lance knew that monsters were real. He had fought more than his fair share of beasties in his travels, both human and inhuman alike.

Still, despite everything he had experienced, it was not impossible to shock him.

He thought he had seen it all.

Then rock creatures bleeding molten lava walked out of the walls right in front of him.

They were terrifying. Blackened rock cracked and popped with each move the creatures made. Lava as fiery red as a hotrod and hot like the volcano they stood upon. Technically, inside of as they were in a cave. The lava boiled beneath the surface as it was compressed between moving stone limbs, dripping to the cavern floor with tiny sizzling plops.

The temperature inside the cavern continued to rise.

"I knew it," Simon Prentiss muttered next to Lance.

"No time to take a victory lap," the pilot told his childhood friend, wiping the pouring sweat out of his eyes. "We have got to go!"

"No place to go, boss," Buck Tellonger said, pointing toward the cavern's entrance where three rock creatures stood, lava dripping from their bodies and pooling around their feet.

"Well, this day just keeps getting better and better, don't it?" Lance said. "I'm open to suggestion."

"Retreat," Buck offered, pointing toward an opening in the wall the rock creatures were building around them.

"That's not out, buck! That'll take us deeper into the cave!"

"Anything's got to be better than here, right?"

"I wouldn't count on it!" Lance said. "Still, we don't seem to have many other options, do we?"

"Nope."

"Damn."

"What about The Overlord and his men?" Buck pointed toward the men nearby.

Two of The Overlord's agents were down, presumably at the hands of the Warriors of Hades. They were covered in lava, dead and scorched. The other two agents were firing on the lava men as they retreated toward the cavern entrance, but to no effect.

The Overlord, himself, had backed up behind them, also shooting aimlessly at the creatures out of myth. If they could stay ahead of the rock men, they had a chance to escape.

The Crown of Gengis Kai had slid to a rest on the cavern floor, the lava moving around it as though to keep it safe or in fear of getting too close.

"We need to get the crown," Simon said.

"Not in this lifetime, pal," Lance said pointedly. "We've got to get moving!"

"But we can't just abandon it!"

"Oh yes we can," Lance said.

"But…"

"Lead the way, Buck," Lance told his co-pilot. "Time to go, Simon!"

Grabbing Simon by the arm, Lance led him through the only escape hatch they had, which wasn't much of one. The heat off of the rock creatures was intense. The nearest one reached for them, as if to grab them and halt their escape.

It missed, but Lance Star felt his arm begin to blister.

"Go!" he shouted, pushing them onward.

The tunnel was dark ahead. The only light came from the reflected red off of the lava that was oozing out of the walls. The heat was tremendous and only getting worse.

When they reached a bend in the tunnel, they understood why.

Before them sat a giant pool of lava.

Unlike the molten earth behind them, this lava stood stationary in a pool with small fires scattered across its surface and ripples of heat radiating above it.

"Dead end," Buck said.

"Poor choice of words," Lance said.

"But accurate. What do you want to do, boss?"

"No way around it," Lance said of the lake of fire. "Two choices."

"Both bad," Simon said.

"We go back… or we die here," Lance said.

"Perhaps I can propose a third option," a gravelly voice said from the darkness.

Lance was wrong.

There were still plenty of things in this world that could surprise him.

This was one.

The rock creature stood in front of them. It made no move to threaten or stop them from backing away. If he had to describe it, Lance would have said that the creature was patient, almost demure. At least so much as a rock creature with lava for blood could be.

"Who are you?"

The rock creature chuckled. The sound was rough, like two rough stones grinding against one another.

"My name is unimportant," the rock man said. "You have trespassed on our sovereign soil. This is in direct violation of our treaty."

"Treaty?"

Lance was confused. He looked from Buck to Simon, who both shook their heads. They were as lost as he was, although he could see Simon's wheel begin to spin.

"Simon?"

Simon snapped his fingers. "You're one of the Warriors of Hades, aren't you?"

"Warriors of Hades?" The rock man ran a granite hand along the side of his head, adding more rock grinding on rock noise to the echo. "Your words are strange."

"Don't you see?" Simon told Lance, grabbing his friend by the arm. "The stories about the crown. In every version of the story I've ever heard, Gengis Kai used the crown to fight the Warriors of Hades."

"This is no time for myth, Professor," Buck said, his eyes focused on the rock creature.

"It's the perfect time," Simon countered. "There are variations in every story about the battle between Gengis Kai and the Warriors of Hades, but there are constants in ever telling of the legend. One of those constants is the battle on this island. They fought here... on Magnapor."

"But it wasn't called that then, was it?" Lance offered.

"No. In those days, this island was basically just the volcano," Simon explained. "Where we're standing now is the original island. The rest of it is built upon the cooled magma from the volcanic eruption that started all those hundreds and hundreds of years ago."

"So?"

"These guys made this island," Simon exclaimed at the discovery. "In every version of the legend of Gengis Kai, the volcano erupts while he's fighting these guys."

"Your friend speaks true," the rock man said. "My people are responsible for this place. We have a great responsibility."

"What responsibility?"

"Removing the sentry has released the enemy."

"Okay, this is getting too out there even for me," Buck said. "We need to go. Now!"

Lance held up a hand to stop his friend.

"Hold up, Buck. I think I understand."

"You do?"

"Maybe. Hang tight a second," Lance said.

"Is this island... this volcano... your home?"

"This place is where I exist," the rock man said.

"But you haven't always existed here, have you?"

"No."

Lance looked at Simon. "You said something about this Kai guy sailing across the ocean, looting and pillaging. He was a pirate, no?"

"That's always been my belief," Simon said.

"Gengis Kai came here after hearing about a powerful enemy, creatures he described as large and human-like with lava burning beneath rock-like shells. Everything they touched burned."

"That sounds right."

"These guys?" Lance said, pointing.

"Yes."

"Does the name Gengis Kai mean anything to you?" Lance asked the rock man.

"It means key."

"So, you knew him?"

"The name is... familiar."

"He fought your people, this key?"

"Yes. At first."

"And after?" Lance pushed.

"After?"

"What happened when your fight finished?"

"The key's eyes were opened."

Lance looked to Simon and Buck, who both shrugged.

"I don't understand. His eyes were opened to what?"

"The greater enemy. Once he saw the true enemy, the key joined my people to save this place."

"You worked together?"

"We became allies against a greater threat."

"I know I'm going to regret asking this," Lance said. "But what greater threat?"

"The enemy who lies beneath us."

"Are you buying any of this garbage, boss?" Buck asked.

"It makes as much sense as anything else I've heard today."

Simon snapped his fingers again.

"You're sentries, aren't you?"

"We are guardians of the key."

"Simon?" Lance asked.

"I think I'm starting to get a clear picture," Simon said. "All of the writing about the battle was either second hand, stories repeated over and over through the centuries, but they all started from a distance. Kai's pirates watched the battle from the sea, remember? What if they weren't watching Kai die fighting? What if they saw him working with these guys? Warriors of Hades was a name given them by the pirates. No one who told the stories ever met them."

"Are you telling me these Rock Men from the Earth's Core are the good guys?" Buck said, clearly not buying it.

"Tell us what happened," lance said.

"The great enemy awoke from its long imprisonment. As the guardians, our responsibility was to keep the enemy at bay. The key's arrival caused our concentration to shift and the enemy awoke."

"The volcano erupted," Simon said, filling in the blanks.

"And that's how the enemy escaped?" Lance added.

"Yes." The rock man nodded. "This is the only way in or out for the enemy."

"It's the crown," Simon said. "The crown is the key. Not Gengis Kai."

Both Lance and Buck looked at him to continue.

"Don't you see?" Simon said. "He called Gengis Kai the key and we found him sitting on that polished throne out there. He was still wearing the crown."

"The crown was boobytrapped," Buck said. "When The Overlord moved it, the lava started pouring in."

"Boobytrapped?" Simon asked. "Or a key keeping an eruption at bay?"

"You think the crown is what's keeping the volcano from erupting?" Lance said. "It's keeping the enemy, the lava, at bay! Is that even possible?"

"Last I saw, Kai's remains were still sitting on the throne. The crown was the only thing moved. The Overlord removed the key to this prison and the prisoner is ready to make a break for it."

"Is that it? We get the crown back in place and the shaking stops?" Buck asked.

"If the enemy has not escaped its fiery prison, the key will once more seal the exit."

"Then why didn't you just put it back instead of coming after us?" Buck asked.

"Good question. Simon?"

The professor shrugged.

"The key is a construct of your world," the rock man said. "It is as deadly to my kind as it is to the enemy beneath. We can no more touch it than he without becoming trapped by its power."

"Well, that's just terrific," Buck muttered.

"And if we return the key, you'll let us walk out of here?" Lance asked, ignoring his co-pilot's sarcasm.

"You will be free to return to your world."

Lance blew out a breath while he weighed their options, of which there were surprisingly few. Hands on hips, he nodded. The decision was made.

"Let's go grab ourselves a key, gentlemen," Lance said as if it were the most normal of tasks.

"I hope nobody changed the locks," Buck muttered as he fell into step behind his friend.

13.

Buck Tellonger was not overly excited by their odds of success.

The cavern had grown even hotter since Buck was last there along with Lance Star and his friend, Professor Simon Prentiss. When they left, lava had slowly begun to pour into the room, filling the cracks and holes first before slowly spreading toward the exit. Nearby, the rock men they had come to know as the Warriors of Hades, a name given to them by the history books, stood at the perimeter of the cavern trying to corral the flowing molten rock.

When he had last seen them, Buck believed they were there to keep them from escaping. In fact, they were doing everything in their power to hold back the lava flow, using their own granite bodies to alter the flow of the molten earth. Buck, along with people throughout history, had made assumptions about the nature of these creatures of myth.

It shamed him to realize how wrong those assumptions had been. He had judged the Warriors of Hades on their look at the name given to them by others who had made similar assumptions. It was a vicious cycle.

"Looks like The Overlord and his goons beat a hasty retreat," Lance Star said, noting the lack of the man who had come at them at gunpoint.

Sure enough, the man who ran the island of Magnapor had taken his surviving secret police officers and exercised the better part of valor.

"Just proves he's smarter than we are," Buck joked, only partly serious.

Lance gave him a curious look, then let out a laugh. "You're probably right," he said around peals of laughter.

Over the years they had flown together, Lance Star and Buck Tellonger had travelled the world, fought despots and dictators, battled skilled pilots in the air and on the ground, faced off against scavengers, smugglers, and pirates, and ran afoul of things that were hard to accurately explain even to the most open-minded of folks. Standing in a cave filling up with lava in the middle of an erupting volcano while surrounded by sentient rock men and trying to rescue a hat might seem a little strange to your average person.

For the Sky Rangers… it was just another Tuesday.

"What's the plan, boss?" Buck asked.

"We need to get that crown back," Lance Star said, pointing across the cavern to the section of floor not covered with lava.

"Easier said than done," Buck told him. "You know how hot that stuff is we got to cross?"

"Not as hot as it's going to be when this cavern fills up with it."

Lance looked around. The cavern was large and contained raised and lowered ledges, rocky outcroppings, and more nooks and crannies than he could count. Streams of molten lava, burning red and yellow flowed down the cavern walls from newly formed cracks in the tunnel walls. Waves of heat radiated off the floor.

Sweating profusely, Lance felt the first wave of lightheadedness. The heat would overtake all of them soon.

They had to act fast.

"Stay here," he told his friends.

"What are you planning to do?" Simon Prentiss asked.

"We need that crown," Lance said as it was the most normal thing. "I'm going to get it."

"There's no way you can survive that heat," Buck Tellonger added.

"No choice."

"Perhaps, I can assist you," the rock creature said. "My people regulate the heat of our surroundings to nourish and strengthen ourselves."

"How does that help us?"

"We can absorb a small fraction of the heat from this chamber for a short time while, allowing you to safely cross."

"Seriously?" Simon asked.

"We can only limit the heat. We cannot remove it."

"I'll take every advantage I can get," Lance said.

"It will be done."

"Then, I guess I'm ready when you are."

"We have begun," the rock man said. "You may begin."

"Be careful, boss."

"Oh, I think we're way past careful, Buck," Lance said offhanded. "If things go belly up, you know what to do, right?"

"I'll make sure he gets out," Buck said.

Lance nodded.

There were open spaces in the floor, raised sections that the lava flow had not reached yet. Lance clocked each one of them. The plan formulating in his pilot's brain was simple enough. He would leap to the first open space, hoping not to burn himself or, worse yet, fall into the lava and be flayed alive. If his new rock-covered ally was correct, the effect would be somewhat minimized. Otherwise, he would never be able to make the leap over the molten liquid without blistering his skin.

"Here goes nothing."

Normally, the pilot kept in shape. He ran the perimeter of Star Field every morning before starting his workday at Lance Star. Inc. On occasion, he hit the weights with the other Sky Rangers after they turned one of the empty rooms off of the maintenance bay into a workout room. He was in tip top form on most days.

This was not most days.

The oppressive heat was taking its toll. Sweat poured off of him in waves, creating moments of lightheadedness and nausea.

And that was before he leapt headlong out of the proverbial frying pan and into the blistering hot oven.

A successful jump took Lance to the first clearing, a section of floor that rose a couple of inches higher than its surroundings.

He wobbled on landing but kept his footing and remained upright.

Lance took a moment to find his next island in the lava.

He jumped.

Lance stumbled upon landing and tipped off balance, landing on his knees before he steadied himself.

The heat buffeted him from all sides.

The crown was two more jumps away.

Of course, then I have to get back, he realized.

The next jump was close and relatively easy.

The last one… well, let's just say the last one was going to be tough.

Lance calmed himself, mentally preparing himself for the leap. The distance was too great for a standing jump so he decided to get as much of a running start as he could, though there was barely enough room for more than three steps.

It would have to be enough.

Lance made his move, poured on the speed, and hurled himself in the direction of the crown.

He landed hard, the toe of his boot snagging the lava and splattering small droplets onto the riser.

He fell forward and came up in a roll before stopping just inches from the edge.

The heat from the lava was intense at this distance.

Slowly, he got to his feet, but needed a moment to steady himself. The extreme temperature was quickly sapping his strength.

Move your tail rudder, Star! he told himself. *No time for lollygagging!*

Lance touched the crown with his finger, making sure that it was not too hot to hold before he scooped it up in his hands. He hadn't thought to bring gloves but there was a back-up plan in case. If the crown was too hot, he could have torn strips from his shirt if need be. Surprisingly, the crown was cool to the touch and he held it easily.

The crown was surprisingly ordinary, all things considered. Lance took a moment to inspect it. The crown was thin, a metal beaten roughly into shape by primitive tools that left it pockmarked and not smooth by any stretch. Gold had been plated onto it in a way that reminded the pilot of dipping it into a vat of gold and allowing the excess to drip off of the crown. A few ornate inscriptions decorated the crown along with a few choice gems. From a strictly monetary standpoint, the crown wasn't really worth all that much.

Up until now, the crown's intrinsic value came solely from its historical context.

Now, Lance understood that the crown was much more valuable as a key.

What surprised him was that the palm fronds that decorated the crown had not wilted in the heat. He wondered if they were made of the same metal as the crown and painted to appear to be flora, but no. He felt the leaves between his fingers. They were real and still alive after all this time.

How is that possible?

There was no time to ponder the question. The lava levels were rising. If he had any plans to get back to safety, then he had to move quickly. From the far edge of the cavern, kept safe by the rock creatures, Buck and Simon shouted warnings to Lance to pick up the pace.

The ace pilot retraced his path, leaping over the small rivers of lava, thankful that the rock creatures were able to keep the temperature lowered so he wouldn't blister and burn as he crossed. It was still hot, but he could handle the artificial sunburn it was giving him easier than he could broken, blistered skin.

At the last stop on his return trip, Lance changed direction. The polished black stone throne remained untouched by the lava, even though it was in one of the lower elevations of the cavern. He had no idea I this was the doing of his new rocky friends or if something in the throne repelled the super-heated magma.

At the end of the day, it really didn't matter.

Lance leapt over a river of lave and landed in the clear, once again crumpling to the floor upon landing. Even with the assistance of his new friends, the heat in the cavern was nearing critical levels. Lance was in great shape, but he was still only human and there were limits to the amount of stress his body could endure.

He was nearing the threshold of his tolerance.

"Lance?" Buck shouted.

The pilots pushed himself up to his knees and held up a hand to keep his friend back. Lance knew Buck Tellonger well. He was a bulldog of a man, afraid of nothing, and loyal to his friends. There was no doubt that the man would throw himself in front of a bullet for any of his friends, probably even for a stranger. If Lance hadn't let him know he was okay, Buck would have leapt over the lava to be at his side.

Lance appreciated that his friend wanted to help, but Buck's mission was clear. If anything happened, it was Buck's job to make sure Simon made it out safely.

Studying the throne, Lance couldn't see anything that resembled technology that could stop the very imminent eruption of the volcano. The mummified remains of the man history referred to as Gengis Kai sat slumped on the throne, his dead eyes staring out int nothingness.

"I guess sometimes you just have to go on faith," Lance said before placing the crown once more on top of the head of Gengis Kai.

From somewhere beneath him, Lance heard a loud CLANG! like steep doors snapping shut.

Almost instantly, the shaking stopped, the lava flow slowed, then stopped.

Miraculously, the molten streams cooled quickly, filling the cavern with steam.

"I can't believe that worked," Lance said, letting out the breath he didn't realize he had been holding.

"Balance has been restored," the rock creature said. "The key is once again in place and the enemy is secured. Both your world and ours are safe once more."

"How is this possible?" Simon Prentiss asked the guardian. "Please, you have to explain…"

"No, he doesn't," Lance said now that he was safely returned to his group. "Trust me, Simon. There are some things it is better off not knowing. You have to believe me on this."

"You can't just expect me to walk away from this, Lance! Don't you see? This is it! This is the find of a lifetime! Your father died trying to locate this place!"

"That's right," Lance said, staring directly into his friend's face. "This damned crown has already cost me a father. Please don't let it cost me a friend as well."

"But…"

"You know it exists, Simon. You've seen the crown with your own eyes. You've seen Gengis Kai's burial chamber. You can amend the history books."

"With rock monsters and ancient enemies kept prisoner under a volcano?"

Lance's face scrunched. "Yeah. That part might be a hard sell. Just leave that part out."

"Just leave it out?" Simon balked. "That's not how science works, Lance!"

"Welcome to the Sky Rangers, professor," Buck joked. "Oh, the stories we can tell you that never made it into a mission briefing."

"I can't just leave without asking them…" Simon continued.

"Asking who?" Lance asked.

That was when Simon realized that the guardians were gone. They had silently returned to their guard stations beneath the surface.

"Dammit!"

"I'm sorry, Simon," Lance said.

"What do we do now?"

"I think our best bet is getting out of here," Lance said. "I don't know about you guys, but I've had all the steam bath I can stand."

"You'll get no argument from me, boss," Buck said and started toward the exit. "Fresh air sounds great right about now."

"I wouldn't get too comfortable, if I were you, Buck," Lance said as they stepped out into the humid island air. The breeze, as warm as it was, still felt cool compared to the air inside the cavern.

"Why not?" Simon asked.

"Don't forget, the volcano and rock men weren't our only problems," Lance reminded him. He pointed toward the horizon and the small dots that pockmarked the sky.

"What's that?" Simon wondered aloud.

Lance and Buck immediately recognized them for what they were.

"Airplanes," Buck said. "The Overlord's men?"

"That would be my guess, Buck. Fighter planes," Lance agreed. "We need to get to the plane before they get here. We need to go! Now! Run!"

Exhausted, the three men found the strength to make a run for their plane. Lance did a quick calculation in his head while on the move. There was a very good chance they wouldn't reach their plane before the planes reached them, much less get in the air before the attack run started.

Suddenly, the volcanic eruption didn't seem so bad.

15.

"Time to hustle, gents!"

By the time Buck Tellonger dropped into the pilot's seat of the cargo plane, the attack had already begun. Four planes showing the colors of Magnapor Island's Overlord, shades of green to denote the tyrant's capitol the locals referred to as the Emerald City, were inbound on approach. The man was nothing if not egotistical. The planes were heavily armed and bore down on the volcano, the airplane parked nearby, and the two men running from one to the other.

While Lance Star hung back to help his friend, Professor Simon Prentiss to the plane, Buck sprinted ahead so he could have her ready to fly when his friends boarded. Prentiss was a brilliant archaeologist, smart, studious, and brimming with knowledge. What he wasn't, however, was an athlete. He was in sorry shape and easily winded. He had even tripped and fallen twice.

After the events of the past day or so, they were all starting to run out of steam, even Lance, who was in decent shape.

"Come on! Just a little farther," Lance told his friend as they ran. "Move your feet, Simon! We've got to go!"

The whine of an engine filled the sky and Lance pushed Simon to the ground a second before machine gun fire chewed up the area just in front of them as one of the enemy planes strafed the area. They were lucky that, in haste to get to them first, the pilot overflew the target and missed. Lance doubted they would be so lucky on the next pass.

The plane pulled up on a high arc, ready to come around for another pass, but not wanting to get in the way of the next plane's attack run.

"We're sitting ducks out here, Simon! Time to run!"

Lance pushed Simon onward. This time, the professor did not argue.

More bullets tore into the ground nearby, gouging out pieces of hardened molten rock and the sand that covered it. The air filled with dust and debris.

Lance Star pulled the weapon from his belt and fired off six shots at the plane passing by overhead. He knew it was an empty gesture. Even if he hit it, there was no way he was going to damage the plane enough to bring them down with a handgun fired from the ground, but he hoped the pilots in those planes wouldn't know that. If it bought them a few extra moments, it was worth the wasted ammo.

He also needed to buy Buck time to get the plane airworthy.

The cargo plane was just ahead. As Simon ran toward it, Lance popped his last magazine into the gun and stopped to face down the next approaching plane.

He squeezed off shots until the chamber was empty.

The pilot of the attack plane veered off course. With his firing solution altered, his field of fire went wide and missed the crazy American pilot by a mile... so to speak.

Simon was already climbing aboard when Lance reached the ladder. He took the steps two at a time and pulled the ladder into the plane behind him before sealing the hatch.

"We're in, Buck!" he shouted. "Let's go!"

"We're gone!"

Before he even got the words out, Buck Tellonger had the plane moving. Lance and Simon grabbed onto the side seats and held on tight as the plane bounced and bobbed over the uneven terrain as they worked to pick up speed for takeoff.

"Hold on!" Buck shouted.

Bullets peppered the cargo plane's hull like angry raindrops attacking a metal roof. A few of the offending projectiles burst through like infuriated bees. A couple of shots ricocheted inside the cargo space. Lance and Simon dove for cover.

"Come on, Buck…" Lance muttered as he wrapped the seatbelt strap around his arm to keep from being thrown about the cargo area. Unlike dice in a cup, there was no chance he or Simon would roll anything but snake eyes.

"Hang on, Simon!" he shouted. "Hang on!"

The plane shook beneath him to the point it felt like it was going to fly apart at the seams. Lance knew better, of course. The team back at Star Fields built their birds tough and sturdy. Lance Star's planes could take a pounding and keep on flying.

At least that's what the press releases always said.

All part of the business side of things.

Lance understood that no plane was perfect. He had walked away from more than a few hard landings, which is pilot talk for crashing. Dogfights were a completely different matter. Not only did you have to have the better plane, but the pilot's skill made all the difference.

Until he was able to stand, Lance was trapped in the cargo hold and of no help to Buck.

Then, as suddenly as the thought hit him, the plane defied gravity and parted company with Mother Earth for trip to the heavens. Buck had gotten them in the air, but that was only half the battle. There were still enemy planes on their tail.

Another burst of gunfire peppered the plane, illustrating that very point vividly.

Once he freed himself from the entangled straps, Lance made his way quickly to the stairs leading up to the cockpit. As he climbed the four steps up, he took a moment to check on Simon.

The professor gave him a thumbs up.

"Stay strapped in!" Lance shouted. "Things might get hairy!"

"Might?" Simon echoed.

He couldn't be certain, but Simon thought he heard his friend laugh at that as he slipped through the hatch.

In the cockpit, Buck Tellonger worked the yoke like the combat veteran he was, performing maneuvers honed over countless hours of training and practical combat all the while chewing on a disgusting, fat, unlit cigar. Buck was an air ace, one of the top combat pilots living today. Despite the danger all around them, Buck was also having the time of his life.

Lance dropped into the copilot seat and strapped in.

"Weapons coming on-line," Lance said as soon as he was in place.

"Hurry up, Lance! This bloke's gettin' on my last nerve!"

"Keep your shirt on, Buck," Lance said calmly, as though they were not in a fight for their lives.

"I'll get you lined up. Ready..." Buck said. "Bandit at two o'clock. I'm adjusting… and fire."

Lance squeezed the twin triggers and opened fire on the enemy plane.

He scored a direct hit. Smoke immediately poured from the plane as it lost control. The pilot fought for altitude, but it was a losing battle. The plane was going to crash.

"Eject," Lance muttered.

The pilot did not listen.

The plane plowed into the side of the volcano at top speed, ripping into the hard-packed wall before erupting into flames, the explosion sending flame and smoke billowing into the air.

Lance and Buck held their breath. They were both thinking the same thing.

Will the explosion trigger an eruption?

Thankfully, the volcano refused to play.

"One down," Lance said. "Find me our next contestant, Buck."

"You got it, Boss."

Lance watched through the window as the enemy plane swung wide to realign for another attack. Buck took the plane into an arc that successfully mimicked the other pilot's trajectory. Meanwhile, the enemy pilot's friend, was coming around to flank them. No matter which target Lance focused on, the plane was going to take a hit. *Thank goodness we build 'em tough*, he thought.

"This is going to be tight, boys," Buck called out a warning. "Brace yourselves!"

Once the targeting was lined up, the ace pilot opened up with the guns and sent streams of bullets into the plane's starboard wing, chopping it to pieces. Thick, oily smoke trailed out of the plane as it spiraled into the ground much like his friend had moments ago.

"Splash two!"

Before they could enjoy the victory or line up their next shot, another enemy plane opened fire on the plane.

Buck took it into a dive to avoid taking fire.

He was only partly successful.

Bullets peppered the hull, knocking new dents and dings they would have to bang back out once they got this baby back home to Star Field.

"Hold onto your hats, boys!" Buck shouted. "This might get a little bumpy!"

The ground was coming up to them hard and fast. If Buck miscalculated by even a fraction of a second, they would hit the ground at top speed. It would be the kind of impact where there were no bodies left to recover. Buck was as skilled a pilot as any Lance Star had ever met, but they were all exhausted, the plane shot up, and Buck had recently taken not one, but two beatings from The Overlord's not-so-secret police.

All of this made Lance a touch nervous.

He need not have worried.

At the last moment, Buck jerked the yoke hard and pulled up out of the dive into a steep arc skyward, narrowly avoiding the hard deck by a matter of feet. With all of the damage the plane had taken, they heard rivets pop and metal strain as they gained altitude, but she held together. Lance Star, Inc. built their planes to take a lot of punishment, but even Lance was beginning to think they were pressing their luck.

The plane that had been chasing him did not fare as well.

Unable to pull out of the dive in time, the pilot slammed into the ground at top speed.

The plane exploded on impact.

That's three down...

The cargo plane continued to climb.

"Buck..." Lance said as pressure increased on his chest.

"I know," the pilot said.

"Buck..."

"I know," he repeated through grit teeth.

"Buck..."

"Now!"

Buck came out of the climb and leveled off. For just the briefest of moments, they felt weightless, held in place only by their seatbelts. It was an odd sensation.

Then everything returned to normal and Buck took her back down quickly, angling around so they could find their final target before the other pilot could get a firing solution on them.

Midway into their descent over the island, the other plane came into view. It was an easy target and Lance opened fire on it.

The enemy plane exploded in a ball of fire as Buck piloted them around the falling debris and headed out toward sea, putting as much distance between them and the Emerald City as possible.

"Waa-Hoo!" Buck shouted in triumph. "Now that's some mighty nice shootin', partner!"

Lance clapped Buck on the shoulder, smiling proudly.

"That wasn't a bad bit of flying either, Buck, ol' boy."

"We aim to please, boss."

Exhausted, Lance leaned back in the co-pilot's seat and breathed a sigh of relief.

"How's your friend doing back there?"

Lance looked back to check on Simon Prentiss, who was sitting in the cargo area on a bench along the hull.

"You still in one piece back there?"

"I'll live," Simon said.

"I'm sorry you didn't get your prize."

"It's okay, Lance. I got to see it with my own eyes. I held it in my own hands. That is more than any other archaeologist has done in our lifetime."

"I think my old man came close though," Lance said.

"I think he did too," Simon agreed. "Part of me wishes he had found it."

"And the other part?" Lance prodded.

Simon Prentiss smiled and shrugged.

"Welcome to the history books, pal," Lance told him. "I figure you'll get a book or two out of this."

"At least," Simon beamed. "Maybe a whole series. I'm thinking lecture tours, book signings..."

"Maybe a motion picture?" Lance added.

"Now there's an idea," Buck chimed in. "Whoever they get to play me better have one handsome mug. They kinda broke the mold when they made this face."

They laughed.

"Thanks for helping me do this, Lance," Professor Prentiss said.

"Anytime, pal. That's what friends are for."

Simon smiled, then added, "That was some... ah... amazing flying, Mr. Tellonger."

"It's even more fun when people aren't shooting at ya," Buck said with a laugh.

"I can imagine."

"You ever get the urge to go up for a joyride, just holler."

"I'll keep that in mind," Simon said, suddenly nervous about the prospect.

"What's our next step, boss?" Buck asked. "You want to go back there and get into it with The Overlord or keep flying? There's no way their letting us land at that airfield again."

"Right now, I'm too tired to even think about The Overlord," Lance said. "Besides, as much as I hate to admit it, he is the rightful government of Magnapor, corrupt though he may be. He's got the law and firepower on his side. Besides, he ain't going anywhere. I'd bet dollars to donuts we'll get into it with him some other time."

"You sure?"

"Oh, yeah. We'll be back here eventually," Lance said. He even sounded exhausted. "Let's go home before The Overlord sends any more of his goons after us."

"Best plan I've heard all day," Buck said.

"Take us home, Buck," Lance said as he leaned back and closed his eyes and drifted off to sleep.

Buck Tellonger set a safe cruising altitude and pointed the plane in the direction of the good ol' U.S. of A. They would have to stop off in Hawaii to refuel, but Buck always enjoyed a visit to paradise. Maybe he could convince the boss to let them stay a day or two for a well-earned vacation. It had been too long since Buck had danced with an island girl at a luau. He just hoped this volcano stayed quiet for the duration of their visit.

As the plane flew off into the sunrise, Lance Star got the best nap of his life.

The End.
Until next time.

Lance Star: Sky Ranger will return.

TAKING BACK THE CROWN
REVISITING AN UNFINISHED TALE TURNS INTO AN ALL-NEW ADVENTURE
AN ESSAY BY BOBBY NASH

We all have them.

That story you had to abandon or cut short, a storyline that had to be scrapped or retooled. If you've written for any length of time then it will probably happen to you too. I've lost count of the number of times I've had to readjust midstream. Often, though, something amazing comes out of it.

That's what happened with Lance Star and the Crown of Gengis Kai. Or was that Ghengis? Genghis? I spelled it all three ways before I finally settled on one particular spelling. It happens. This is why we edit. Ha! Ha!

James Burns and I have been friends for a number of years. We are often table neighbors at the one day Atlanta Comic Convention show that happens four times a year. We have similar inspirations and have worked together a few times now, most notably on the Lance Star: Sky Ranger one shot comic book titles "One Shot!" I know. I know. I'm not as clever as I think I am. Ha! Ha! We also worked on some shorter pieces for a couple of anthology comics James put together. You should absolutely check out James' site and pick up some of his comics. You won't be disappointed. Links can be found on his bio page.

We were talking about comic strips when the idea of this story came about. I love comic strips. There's something unique about this form of storytelling, much like telling a serialized novel, which is what the novella you hold in your hand was originally written. More on that in a bit. James agreed to do the art and I started writing.

A few strips into things, a scheduling conflict came up. It happens. As a result, the strip, which was originally intended to run twenty-eight (I think) pages was reduced to ten. We wrapped things up quickly and, since we didn't have the showdown in the volcano, Lance and Simon actually manage to escape with the crown, unlike in this story.

The original comic strip story has been added to this volume and you can read it in a couple of pages. I cut the pages up to better fit this paperback format, much like the collections I read as a kid that did a similar formatting trick. I thought that was a good way to add those to this volume. You can see the original, color strips in their proper format at my website and the Lance Star: Sky Ranger website. Links/ads are also coming up.

The story of Lance Star and the Crown of Gengis Kai plays with all kinds of pulp tropes. There's action, larger than life heroes, dastardly mustache-twirling villains, pirates, volcanoes, lava monsters, and more. As a writer, these type of stories remind me of playing make-believe as a kid. Anything goes and everything works. There's a lot of fun to be found in that freedom.

The notes for the original comic strip version are long gone. I tried looking for them with little success. Most of the story I recalled from memory, but some pieces I just made up on the fly. Not allowing Simon to successfully remove the crown was one of those, but I think it adds an extra layer to the story.

Lance Star and his Sky Rangers were my first introduction to writing what has become affectionately referred to as New Pulp. Airship 27 Productions published four anthologies featuring four stories each. I have one in each anthology. There's also an ebook that collects my four stories in one single volume. They are big fun and I invite you to check them out.

After the last anthology, I thought I had moved on from Star Field and the pulpy goodness that is writing the Sky Rangers, but like any good character, Lance and the crew won't let me walk away. Over the past couple of years, Lance has had all-new adventures appear in two magazines; Pulp Adventures #32 and Pulp Reality #1. The book you hold in your hand was released originally as a serialized novel on my Patreon page and then later on the New Pulp Heroes site. That's not all. There is more Lance Star: Sky Ranger on the way in the form of a full-length original novel, a comic collection, and more novellas like this one. There may even be a surprise project or two as well.

I love these characters and I am thrilled to continue writing their adventures. I hope you'll join us. It promises to be a wild ride.

For those of you who have been with this project since the serialized days on Patreon, an extra special thank you. I plan to do Lance's next adventure as a serialized book too. Stay tuned.

Stay safe and as always, I'm ready on the flight line.

Bobby
Star Field, NY
(*by way of Bethlehem, GA*)

MEET BOBBY NASH

Bobby Nash is an award-winning author. He's a member of the International Association of Media Tie-in Writers and International Thriller Writers. He occasionally appears in movies and TV shows, usually standing behind your favorite actor. He draws a little too.

Bobby was named Best Author in the 2013 Pulp Ark Awards. Rick Ruby, a character co-created by Bobby and author Sean Taylor also snagged a Pulp Ark Award for Best New Pulp Character of 2013. Bobby has also been nominated for the 2014 New Pulp Awards and Pulp Factory Awards for his work. Bobby's novel, Alexandra Holzer's Ghost Gal: The Wild Hunt won a Paranormal Literary Award in the 2015 Paranormal Awards. The Bobby Nash penned episode of Starship Farragut: Conspiracy of Innocence won Silver Award in the 2015 DC Film Festival. His story in The Ruby Files Vol. 2 "Takedown" won the 2018 Pulp Factory Award for Best Short Story.

His novel, Nightveil: Crisis at the Crossroads of Infinity was named Best Pulp Novel in the 2020 Pulp Factory Awards. In 2020, The Sangria Summit Society awarded the New Pulp Fiction Award to Bobby Nash for his work on Snow Falls and the Snow series.

For more information on Bobby Nash and his work, please visit him at www.bobbynash.com and www.ben-books.com as well as on social media.

MEET JAMES BURNS

James Burns is a graphic designer, animator and comic artist who lives in Athens, Georgia. As a graphic designer for television he created 3D animations for clients such as CNN, TBS and various television stations around the country.

In 2002, he was diagnosed with a detached retina, which threatened his eyesight. After recovering, and at age 45, he wrote and drew his first comic book, Detached about the experience, as well as the fear and doubts that were connected with it.

After that, he created the weekly comic strip Grumbles for Atlanta's Sunday Paper, which ran in print for 6 1/2 years, and online for a total of 12.

James has also created several independently published comics including his graphic novel Daemon Process, his anthology Real Magicalism, the parody Astral Crusader, Speechless, Über-tales, as well as several annual collections of his "Grumbles" strips. His work has also been included in the last several editions of Not My Small Diary.

In 2010 he worked with Bobby Nash on the Lance Star: Sky Ranger comic entitled "One Shot!" His latest work is a graphic memoir called A Life Half-Forgotten. It's all about growing up in Central Ohio suburbia during the 60s and 70s, and deals with the nature of memory.

James' comic work can be found at burnscomics.com.

MEET JAMES BURNS

Artist Self Portrait

SPECIAL THANKS!

No book is created solely in a vacuum and this one is no exception. Big thank you's to James Burns for being my partner on this one and supplying the cover art. Also, Ron Fortier, and Rob Davis, who were there when Lance Star was born.

As always, a HUGE THANK YOU to my Patrons for supporting my work on Patreon, where Lance Star and the Crown of Gengis Kai first appeared as a serialized novella. I appreciate each and every one of you. My Patrons are the best. James Burns (no relation), Robert McIntyre, Lil' John Nacinovich, Sean R. Reid, John Kilgallon, Andrea Judy, Darrell Grizzle, Jack D. Kammerer Jr., Jeff Allen, Caine Dorr, Colin Joss, Adam Messer, Nicole Thomas, David Perlmutter, Brian K. Morris, Jeffrey Hayes, and Michael Stackpole. Rock stars one and all. Your support is appreciated.

JOIN ME ON PATREON TODAY!

WWW.PATREON.COM/BOBBYNASH

THE ORIGINAL COMIC STRIP
BY BOBBY NASH AND JAMES BURNS

The title was changed after this was originally released.

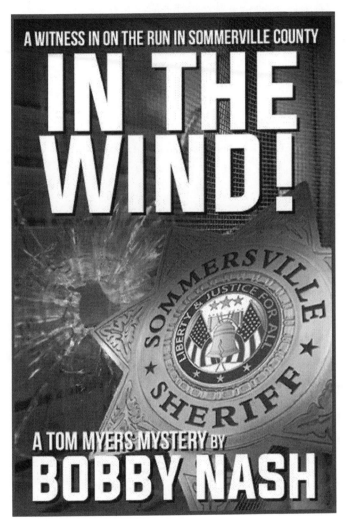

ALSO BY BOBBY NASH

Evil Ways
Deadly Games!
Earthstrike Agenda
Domino Lady: Money Shot
Alexandra Holzer's Ghost Gal:
The Wild Hunt
Snow Falls
Snow Storm
Snow Drive
Snow Trapped
Snow Star
Suicide Bomb
Nightveil: Crisis at the
Crossroads of Infinity
Fightcard: Barefoot Bones
Adventures of Lance Star: Sky Ranger
85 North
Sanderson of Metro
In The Wind – A Tom Myers Mystery
The Ruby Files (Vol. 1 & 2)
Domino Lady: Sex as a Weapon

And many more. Visit Bobby at
www.bobbynash.com for a full list.

Made in the USA
Columbia, SC
05 May 2023

16085619R00098